I0702868

JUST ONE *night*

Author of the Kiss Me Crazy Series

JAMI ROGERS

To my mom, dad, and sister.
I love you all more and more each day.

Just One Night

Copyright © 2015 by Jami Rogers

All rights reserved.

No part of this book may be reproduced or transmitted in any form or by any means, electronic or mechanical, including photocopying, recording, or by any information storage and retrieval system without the written permission of the author, except for the use of brief quotations in a review.

This is a work of fiction. Names, characters, businesses, places, events and incidents are either the products of the author's imagination or used in a fictitious manner. Any resemblance to actual persons, living or dead, or actual events is purely coincidental.

Editor: Julie Sturgeon, CEOEditor, ceoeditor.com

Copyediting/Proofreading: Casey Dawes, Concierge Self-Publishing, www.ConciergeSelfPublishing.com

Formatting: Jesse Gordon, a Darned Good Book, adarnedgoodbook.com

Newest Formatting by Jami Rogers.

Visit my website: www.authorjamirogers.com

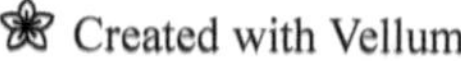 Created with Vellum

JUST ONE *night*

Author of the Kiss Me Crazy Series

JAMI ROGERS

CHAPTER ONE

Last summer …

Sara

I'm fully aware of my own vulnerabilities. I know what I need to do to avoid them and yet, I'm about to be alone in The Black Alcove bar, BA for short, that I manage for my father, with my number one weakness. Logan Parker.

The lock clicks under Logan's fingers after the last two customers are finally out the door. Friday night of finals week is always the busiest night. What better way to celebrate passing finals and the start to summer than with a drink, right?

"I honestly thought those last two guys were never going to leave," Logan says, sauntering behind the bar. He flicks the last of the lights on, and we both squint at the brightness.

"They had so many drinks, I was beginning to think they were going to pass out here," I respond.

It's nearing two thirty in the morning, and I can't speak for Logan, but I'm exhausted and can't wait to crawl into my bed and fall asleep. This was my final semester, too. I'm officially a college graduate—minus knowing my official grades and the fact I'm choosing not to walk with the rest of the class—and although I should be joining other students my age, I'm working.

Work before play is the Connelly way.

My father taught me this motto while he and my mother were splitting up when I was ten. He told me I need to follow it so I don't make the same mistakes he did. Twelve years later, this motto follows me everywhere. The part where my mother left and never came back proves his reasoning accurate. I get the yearly birthday card from her, but that's all and I'm okay with it.

"Did you see the shirt he was wearing?" Logan asks, chuckling as he drains the sinks and begins to scrub them clean.

"Yes! Oh god. It looked exactly like that blue button up you wore every day of junior year."

"I didn't wear it every day."

"Only the ones where you were in class." I laugh, pulling up a seat as he hands me the cash drawer and turns the credit card machine toward me. I punch a few numbers and the receipt of tonight's numbers starts to print.

"Hey, that was a classy shirt. It made me look good, and if I remember right, I was wearing that shirt the day I asked you out."

"Yep, that's right, and you wore it every day that we dated, too."

"I wore different shirts that year."

"Not that I remember."

Logan quickly sprays me with the sink's hose and I squeal when the cold water splashes against my skin.

"Okay, okay, whatever happened to that shirt anyway?" I ask when he tosses me a towel, flashing the grin that tugs every emotion I've ever felt for him. And it's a lot. Especially when I know exactly where said shirt is—in my closet. I was supposed to give it back to him but never got around to it and now ... well, it'd be creepy if I told him I still had it.

"It was ripped and a few of the buttons were torn off—"

"What? You loved that shirt. How did you ruin it?" I ask. I've always been curious to what happened.

"Mark Matheson actually ripped it. The night we broke up, I went to a party out at Wind River field after I left your house and started a fight. It came off somehow during the brawl and I never saw it again."

Those same emotions—joy from what we had, fear of losing him again, and hope that we could one day go back to that—flood back into my chest as I gaze up at him from my seat. His eyes flash to mine briefly before he looks away.

"What do you think would have happened if we hadn't broken up?" he asks. There's a hesitation to his voice, but when his eyes settle on me again, I see fear. He's nervous about my answer.

"Logan, I—"

I can't even finish the sentence because although I've thought of this moment time after time since high school, my heart couldn't take it again. I'll never forget the day Logan told me he couldn't have a girlfriend because his life was just beginning. He would be going away for college and didn't want to continue something he couldn't hold a promise to. That he wouldn't even try broke my heart the way any seventeen-year-old's heart would break. I thought my life was over.

It took almost our entire senior year of high school for us

to go back to the friends we were before dating. I've imagined us starting a relationship again, but I can't lose him the way I did before. Not with the friendship we have now.

"Wait, don't answer that. I just … I want you to know that breaking up with you was one of the biggest mistakes I could have made, and I'd do anything to take it back."

I blink, watching as his eyes bore into my own, and my breathing gets faster. His gaze never breaks its hold as he quickly rounds the bar.

"I'm not asking you to make a decision right now, or even tomorrow or the next day. But I am asking you to think about it."

"Logan, it's been five years. Where is this coming from?"

"Sara, come on, that spark between us—it's always been there. You're the first person I go to with good news, and I know I'm that person for you, too. We flirt more than your average friends should and that's because we've never been just friends. Never. I'm finally speaking up about it."

"Logan—" The words to disagree catch in my throat because he's right.

"Just one night, Sara. That's all I'm asking. Nothing has to happen that you don't want to, but just spend one night with me."

The fact he isn't asking for a commitment is comforting. The fact that this is Logan—the guy who holds my first for every important moment in life, the guy who has held my heart since high school—makes my decision easy.

"Okay," I answer, not considering that he's also the guy who could destroy me. His lips are on mine before I can say anything else. Just one night, that's all I need, too.

CHAPTER TWO

One year later …

Sara

My back rubs against the tree, and when Logan pushes his body against mine, the bark digs into my skin. In this moment, I don't care. I will accept it. I'll even enjoy it. There's zero amount of pain that could keep me from kissing Logan Parker.

The fear of what comes after kissing Logan, is different.

There are only three things in life that terrify me. The first is dying from a freak accident—shark attack, tripping and cracking my head open, or choking while I'm alone come to mind. The second is not being successful. I took college classes in high school and doubled my course load once I was actually attending the local campus just so I could be ahead in my career. My father raised me well, and letting all of that go to waste is a scary thought. And the last thing that scares me, the thing that could ruin me, is committing to someone who will leave me with a broken heart. Committing to Logan Parker to be exact.

The last part was the reason I decided to travel to all the fifty states and to Europe last year. It was a last minute decision, but one night with Logan had me rethinking the two things in life I thought I knew for sure—my choice in career and rekindling a relationship with him. It was like everything I'd worked for the past few years didn't matter anymore and I was about to make a huge commitment with Logan instead of my career. I thought getting away, far away, would make us both forget what it feels like to be together.

Clearly, I was wrong.

I run my hands through his hair and pull him closer. I love the way his body feels against mine. I dreamed of this moment almost every day that I was away.

His lips trail soft and tender kisses from just below my ear down to my chest. Another moan slips past my lips from his touch. The noises I make when I'm with him are uncontrollable. Fighting it has always been pointless from day one.

Logan pulls away, leaving his hands to rest on my hips. He locks a dreamy gaze with mine and my heart starts to race, the way it does every time his eyes are on me. It makes me feel wanted, desired. I imagine I give him the same exact look.

It doesn't help that he's wearing a pair of khaki slacks with a pressed, white, button-down shirt today. Or that his blonde hair is cut short and shining lighter from the heat of the sun, or that no matter where we are, he keeps those bright blue eyes that sparkle focused on me. The fact I know he has an amazing and almost unbelievably firm body underneath all those clothes really tests the control I have over how much I want him right now.

His pleased grin reveals straight, white teeth.

"I don't think we should sneak around anymore, Sara," Logan whispers, moving his hand to mine and pulling me into his arms.

Since I've been back from Europe, sneaking around has been our thing. I left with the idea I wanted space, but I returned with the idea I need Logan. I even had a weak moment and came home to see him for a few days.

Our group of friends; Kelsey, Beth, Logan, Ethan, and myself are close, and I don't want to ruin that, so telling anyone we've started something new isn't at the top of my list. It's been nothing but a few stolen, secret moments together. Moments we never talk about to anyone but each other, not even with Kelsey, my best friend. And I want to tell her so bad.

A part of me likes the idea of sneaking around. It makes everything between us more electrifying. Not knowing what will happen, not planning anything out, just going with whatever emotion I have right then and there makes me feel free. It's the total opposite of everything in my life. Plus, the feeling of being caught gives me such a rush.

Especially right now. We're at my father's house for my twenty-third birthday, and we're hiding in the trees on the side of the house. It's a beautiful, sunny June day and everyone is in the backyard enjoying the barbeque he throws for me each year. Still, anyone could turn the corner and find us.

I love it.

"Sara? Did you hear what I said?" Logan asks, rubbing my arms and hooking his gaze on mine.

"Yes, I did. I'm sorry. I was completely zoning out."

"I could see that." He chuckles.

"If you don't want to sneak around, what do you want?" I ask, mentally crossing my fingers he still wants what he wanted before I left. Me.

His smirk gives me my answer.

"I'm pretty sure you already know."

My heart begins beating faster as I control my body from jumping up and down, or more specifically, onto him. My lack of outward excitement doesn't come off positively. Logan's watching me with a worried expression.

"I know you're scared, but I think it's time we make this official," he says with a hopeful grin. "I was an idiot to let you leave last year without at least asking you to stay. What I want in life isn't going to just fall into my hands. I have to work for it, and working for an 'us' is what I want."

"Okay," I answer.

Logan grips my shoulders and pushes me away at arm's length. He looks me in the eye and a smile I've never seen but love already stretches across his face.

"Okay? As in, okay we're officially a couple?"

"Yep."

My back hits the tree fast and his lips press against mine. I'm not sure if I'm seeing stars because my head hit the trunk or because he's kissing me like I'm his air and he can finally breathe. *He's never kissed me like this before.* His hands start exploring every part of my body, leaving a tingling trail everywhere they touch. A giddy feeling rushes to my core as Logan grips my ass, lifting me until my legs are wrapped around him. With his hands cupping my butt, he holds me there, pressing me against his hips as they grind into mine.

What else has he been holding back?

He breaks away quickly, breathing hard and lowering my feet back to the ground. Before I can tell him I want to keep going, he grabs my hand.

"Come on. We better go before your dad finds me and kills me for sneaking around with you."

I nod and step past him, laughing as he tickles my sides from behind me. I know happiness is written all over my face. This is it. This is the moment I take a risk and begin to conquer one of my biggest fears.

Logan

The sound of Sara's laughter is the most incredible noise I've ever heard. I don't care how whipped I sound when I say it or even think it. I'm lucky as hell she's giving me a second chance. Between my last year of college coming up, a student loan that I'm falling behind on paying, a rent check two months past due, and a sister I've been trying to contact but have heard nothing from, luck is something I haven't had in a while.

I pull Sara back at the waist until she's walking next me. Never letting my hand leave her side, I sneak a glimpse to admire her. Her blonde hair is braided to the side. Her peach summer dress falls just above her knees and flows with each step she takes. The color makes her tan look darker. She isn't wearing any jewelry or shoes, which is odd because this girl loves her accessories.

I watch as a glowing smile never leaves her lips. She squeezes the hand that's tangled with mine as she looks up to me with her light blue eyes. I'm not just quoting a line when I say that she has the most beautiful and breathtaking eyes I have ever seen. They are eyes that twist and break any control I have.

Sara's father's house is at the base of Wind Valley's mountain and is surrounded by tall oak trees, giving it a slight forest look. Her smiling continues as we step past the last tree. I squeeze her tiny figure again as she walks in front of me. At my touch she trips, falling into my shoulder. I turn her upright, facing me. Right then, she does something amazing. She stands on the tips of her toes and presses a gentle kiss to my lips right in front of everyone we know.

Expecting to hear shouts and hollers, we hear nothing. Glancing to the party, I see why. Not a single person is looking our way. Sara's happy smile is still glued in place.

"And all this time we always thought someone would catch us, when really, no one was ever looking," she says, sounding as shocked as I am. We laugh as we join the party.

"Did you know Kelsey and Ethan eloped last month?" I ask, taking a seat at the eight-person metal rectangle patio set. Sara sits on my left knee, resting against me as I wrap my arms around her.

"I might have known that." She smirks, leaning forward to open the closest cooler to us. I never let my hands stray from somehow touching her. She hands me a beer and grabs a Pepsi for herself, flipping the top and taking a drink. It's always amazed me that she practically owns a bar, yet she hardly drinks alcohol. I think I've seen her drink three times in all the years I've known her. "You do know Kelsey is my best friend, right? We don't really keep secrets from each other."

She's lying. She never told Kelsey about last summer. I

would have received some sort of ass chewing from Kelsey if she had. I smile, cocking an eyebrow at her.

"Okay, so there are *some* things we don't share." She laughs.

"Yeah, I thought so," I say, giving her sides another squeeze as she squeals. It feels so good to show her how much I care for her to all our friends.

"So, does this mean you're finally out in the open with all this?" Kelsey says, sitting across from us. Ethan takes the seat next to her with a shit-eating grin on his face, too.

"What do you mean, *finally*?" Sara asks.

"Like we didn't know." Ethan laughs.

"Everyone knew something was going on," Kelsey adds. "We just didn't know what exactly that was."

With her mouth open, Sara looks over her shoulder at me.

"I never said anything"—I raise my hands in surrender form—"swear it."

She rolls her eyes but smiles at the same time.

"Yes, it does," Sara answers at the same time I nod in Ethan's direction.

"It's about freaking time," Ethan says, winking at both of us. "The tension between you two was getting a bit ridiculous."

"Shut up, it was not." Sara laughs.

"Oh it most definitely—"

"If I could please have everyone's attention!"

Sara jumps at the sound of her father's booming voice. He steps through the French doors that lead from his kitchen onto the patio and comes to a stop once he's next to us. Sara stands slowly and I do the same, holding her hand tightly in mine.

"As you all know, I have been working to expand my

business for some time now. It may just be a bar to most of you, but to me it's how I provide for myself and for my daughter, and it brings me such joy to share with all of you today the birthday gift I have for Sara."

I can feel Sara's hand stiffen so I hold on tighter. Her father turns to face us and the excitement falls from his face when he notices my arms wrapped around her. He swallows and looks me in the eye for a brief moment before returning his focus back to Sara.

"Congratulations, dear. We got the place in Colorado, and it's all yours."

Fuck. Maybe luck isn't on my side after all.

CHAPTER THREE

Sara

I've heard the expressions "timing is everything" and "everything happens for a reason." I just thought they were silly because life isn't about luck. If you want something, you go after it and you don't give up. This gift from my father is proof that theory is true. *I'm finally getting my own bar!* First I made a commitment to Logan and now I'm getting what I've been working toward. Today is freaking fabulous.

I let my father finish his speech before I excuse myself and head inside. A smile is plastered to my face as I pour a soda into a plastic cup. Managing the BA has been great, but I never owned it. I've always had to clear everything through my father. Not anymore. *I've got my own bar.* Ah! This day couldn't get any better.

I pass through the kitchen and take a seat on the living room sofa. The room is filled with pictures of me with my parents, most of them with my father. All moments from my accomplishments, everything from spelling bees in elementary to graduating college. I excelled at everything in those years, and I've earned today.

The click of the front door announces a newcomer to the party—someone new I can share my good news with and relive it again.

"Hey, girl, sorry I'm late. I was—Hey, whoa, what's wrong? That's sort of a pitiful smile you got there." The couch dips as Beth sits next to me. Beth Moyer is both a great friend and an employee at The Black Alcove.

"Logan and I are together." I glance up. She's staring me down with her hands folded in her lap. Something about her red hair, white summer dress, and the spark in her emerald eyes reminds me of the Little Mermaid right now.

"That's great," she cheers, clapping her hands.

"My father gave me the bar."

"Wow! Even better."

"In Colorado."

"Oh, shit," she says, every ounce of cheerfulness has left her voice, and my head jerks back at her response.

"What do you mean 'oh shit?'" I ask, curious to why she doesn't she see this as good news.

"You're really asking me that?" Her question makes her sound just as confused.

"Yeah, this is great news. Unless you mean 'oh, shit yes, this is awesome,' I don't think were on the same page."

"Well doesn't owning a bar in Colorado mean you have to move?"

"Yeah, so?"

"So, if you and Logan just started dating, how is that going to work?"

I shrug. "He'll come with me."

"Um, are we talking about the same Logan?"

I never suspected Beth to be the party pooper. Fine, right now isn't the ideal time for Logan to pick up and move, but he'll do it for me. All he has to do it switch schools. A transfer won't be that hard.

"Okay, think about this: if he moves with you, the two of you are going from not even dating to living together. Is that a commitment you want to make?"

"Just because we move doesn't mean we have to live together," I point out. *No need to freak me out with more commitment talk, Beth.*

"If I moved to another state for someone, that's asking for a huge commitment," she adds and I cringe. She really needs to stop using that word.

"Sara, are you okay in here?" Kelsey asks in a gentle voice as she steps into the living room holding her new baby, Clara, in her arms. I glance back and forth between my friends trying to decide if "okay" is the word I would use to describe the outcome of this conversation. Beth is right, if I ask Logan to move, I'm making a bigger commitment than I'm ready to make. Thousands of people make long-distance relationships work every day. Logan and I are no different.

"Yes, everything is great," I say with a stoned expression. And it will be as long as Logan is okay with me leaving without him.

Logan

Fuck.

Just one word says it all. If I had any gut feeling that Sara's father doesn't approve of me, this confirms it. He wants to keep us apart, and I can't believe he's sending her to an entirely different state to do it. I don't come from the same background as them. I didn't grow up with luxuries and money. I didn't and don't have parents who encourage me or believe in me. Parents who love me. All I have is a sister who won't return my letters and Sara. Her father is about to take away something more important to me than myself, and I think he knows it, too.

"Logan."

Ethan's voice pulls me back into reality as he waves a hand in front of my face while everyone else goes about the party like something intense didn't just happen.

"That was a little creepy," Ethan whispers. "It was like you zoned out. I said your name probably ten times. I know you have feelings for Sara, we all do, but your face just told me more than I thought."

"I know," I groan into my hands.

"What are you going to do? You can't let her leave, not now. You two just made this official. Her father is ruining it. I'd be so furious and lost right now."

Furious and lost is right and Ethan would know. He found someone he refuses to imagine his life without, and until this moment, I never knew how that felt.

"Mr. Parker." Sara's fathers clears his throat as he interrupts our conversation. "Could I have a word with you?"

"Yeah, I need to check on Kelsey anyway," Ethan stutters.

There he goes again, rushing off inside the house like a girl. It's good to know I have a friend who can get me to laugh even in an unwanted situation. I push off my knees as I come to a stand in front of Sara's father. Even for a man nearing his late fifties, he towers over me at six foot five with gray hair, and his solid frame for an old guy is intimidating. He pins me with dark eyes and sticks one hand in his tan slacks pocket while the other holds a glass at his lips. Whiskey and water on the rocks, no doubt. I've been a bartender at the BA for a couple years now, and he's never ordered anything different. He nods and points for me to walk with him.

"You know, Logan, in the years I've known you, you've surprised me."

I don't say anything as we stop at the drink table. He pours another drink and offers the glass to me. I take it even though I hate whiskey.

"You've turned out to be a much stronger, more determined, and smarter man than I would have imagined. And with the way my daughter speaks about you, I know I've been wrong about you all these years."

Whoa. How do I respond to that?

"Thank you, sir," I say as we come to a stop just outside the kitchens doors.

"I know I'm making the right decision when I ask you to manage and run The Black Alcove while my daughter is away. I'm not the young and quick man I once was. I need someone this family can trust to fill in where I can't. After last year, calling my brother for help is not something I will ever reconsider. You are the right person for the job, and I believe that you will take care of my business as if it were your own. You salary will be more than doubled, of course." He adds the last part as if it were an afterthought.

Wow.

The entire compliment doesn't go unnoticed, but I focus on the last sentence. I could really use that money. I could have my student loan paid off faster than I expected, my rent would be caught up, and I could start saving for a future with Sara. It would mean staying here apart from Sara, but if anyone understands building a career, it's her.

"Thank you, sir. I'd be happy to—"

"Logan," Sara squeals as she comes through the open doors with a smile bigger and brighter than ever. She doesn't take her eyes off of me as she closes her arms around my neck. I wrap my arms around her waist and hold tight. She kisses me right in front of her father, but I cut it short—I need her father to know I'm serious. That I am all those things he said, that I can take care of his business and show him that I'm someone worthy of his daughter. My only wish is that I could do all that without Sara being hundreds of miles away from me. *Damn Ethan.* He turned me in to sap.

Sara releases her hold, giving me another quick kiss on the cheek before she turns to her father. Right now I want to do more than a quick a kiss on the cheek. I want to be anywhere else. I want her alone. I want to forget that we are going to start our relationship apart from each other. Although she wasn't that sad when she came through those doors, I sure hope she takes my suggestion of our embracing our different career paths well.

"Can I steal him for just a second, Dad?"

"Actually, Sara, dear, before you do that, I want you to know that I've chosen Logan to manage the BA in your absence."

If I'm not mistaken, Sara's shoulders relax with relief.

"Dad, that's—"

"He could run that place in his sleep. And that's why I think it would be in our best interest if he took over."

She nods her head and an ear-to-ear grin touches her lips.

Excited eyes find mine as she throws her arms around my neck.

"Logan, this is fantastic!"

"Yeah, I, uh … I think so too," I reply, hugging her back. *She isn't upset that I'm staying here and she's moving?* "Do you think we could—"

"Isn't Ethan already managing the bar?" Beth chimes in at an unfriendly volume from somewhere behind us. Her confidence to speak to Mr. Connelly this way probably comes from years of being Sara's friend.

"Ethan is … looking into a different career path," Sara's father tells her.

"What, since when?"

"Since he became a father and is about to be a husband, he wants a job that lets him be home at decent hours. It's a very honorable thing to do, and I don't blame him for putting his family first."

As if he knows we're talking about him, Ethan chooses this exact moment to come outside.

"Ethan," Beth says loudly even though he's standing only a few steps away. "Why didn't you tell me you were quitting?"

"You're quitting?" Abby asks in shock as she and Kelsey join him. I didn't even realize Abby showed up. Since she's both a coworker and a friend none of us trust very well, I wasn't aware Sara had invited her. But then again, Sara has the kindest heart of anyone I know, so it shouldn't surprise me. Kelsey and Abby walking together, on the other hand— well, that's not the subject right now.

"I …" Ethan starts then glances franticly between Sara and me.

"Oh … this isn't good," Kelsey says, leaning in Abby's direction. "With Ethan gone, Logan's the only one with enough experience to run the BA, unless Mr. Connelly wants to return. And if Logan takes the position, he won't be leaving with Sara."

"Shit," Beth says and doesn't even try to lower her volume.

Yeah, shit.

"Sara, I think you should get back to your party and you ladies can continue this conversation another time." Her father's tone is clipped.

She stares at her father for a few seconds, then glares at Beth. Our friend's expression shifts quickly, and in all honesty, looks like she's about to cry. Everyone slowly steps away from the circle we've created, leaving Sara and I alone.

Our eyes meet briefly before she reaches for my hand.

"I think we should go," she says, her tone void of any excitement.

I don't say anything because my fear that she's going to end this before it can even begin is strong. And that's the last thing I'm going to let her do.

Sara

I find Logan's hand, yanking hard as I pull him through the house. I grab my purse from the kitchen table and then Logan's truck keys off the foyer table, walking us right out the front door. Logan doesn't say a word as I hand him the keys, pointing to his truck. He still doesn't talk until we're sitting in the parking lot outside my apartment.

Yeah, I'm happy that my father gave my position to

Logan. Happy that it means he won't be coming with me and that I won't have to endure an awkward conversation about why he should stay here. But when Beth started to get defensive, it occurred to me that I should be the one who is mad. I should want Logan to be with me.

"Is everything okay?" Logan asks as he reaches across the truck to hold my hand. My head falls back against the headrest.

"What kind of person does it make me that I want to go to Colorado to open this new bar, but I also want you to stay here and take the opportunity my dad is giving you?"

Logan licks his lips as his head nods. "I'd say that makes you human, strong, and smart for knowing what you want in life."

A small smile tugs at my lips. "But it also means that I'm a horrible girlfriend and I haven't even had that title for twenty-four hours."

"Don't even think that. I think it's great we aren't letting this get in the way of success. You will do your thing there, I'll do mine here, and we can make it work until you get back."

"Yeah, but this was supposed to be it, the perfect time for us to be a couple. Now it's the exact opposite. We may as well wait until I get back before we give this a real shot," I say. I'm already using the bar as an excuse because I'm scared, but I don't want to admit it.

He shakes his head no.

"You know what, we can do this. We can handle distance. Look at everything we've been through. Rockland, Colorado, is what—three hours from here? I'll come down every weekend if I have to. I'll do anything and everything if it means seeing you."

"You can't do that. Not now that we have a live band almost every weekend," I tell him. Ethan worked so hard last year to find different bands to alternate at the BA. I can't let our choice to be together ruin all that.

"Even with the bands." Logan grins. "I'm not the only one who works there, Sara. Every now and then, they will be able to manage a weekend without me."

I blink at his response. Now probably isn't the time to let him know how nervous that idea makes me. I trust everyone who works there—I wouldn't have hired them otherwise—but I also know how they work, and like most normal people, when the boss is away, things go wrong.

"I see your wheels turning, Sara Connelly. You're going to have to calm down on the perfection factor. I might not be as organized or have the experience you do, but I promise I won't let the BA go under in my first week."

I can feel my eyes practically bugging out of their sockets.

"I said I *wouldn't* let that happen." He laughs, unclipping his belt to slide over next to me. He kisses the side of my head.

"I have an idea. What if we took this time apart to grow as a couple and to grow in our careers? Let's take advantage of what we have been given and make the most of it." He places another kiss to my head before he touches his fingers to my chin and turns my face to look at him. "It's ideal for you to move to Rockland because you're going to own a business there, but in real life, you don't have to live there if you don't want to."

I relax into his embrace and let out a deep breath. "How

do you know me so well? How do you know exactly what to say?"

He chuckles. "I wasn't quite finished yet."

I lean back up, tilting my head to the side as I wait for him to go on.

"Your goal while you are there is to loosen up. Don't let things stress you out. Control is your thing, but I think now is a great time for you to learn you can't control everything."

"Hey, I don't control *everything*."

He cocks a brow at me.

"What? I like structure; it's not a bad thing."

"Okay, at least try?" he asks, flashing me a grin.

I roll my eyes. "Fine. What do you get to do?"

"I have to build better structure."

This time, it's me who looks at him suspiciously.

"What? Unlike you, I think structure is suffocating; it can be a bad thing," he says, playfully mocking me.

I punch his arm and he fakes the injury as we laugh.

His lips are on mine before I can say anything else. His tongue slips into my mouth, twirling with my own as his arms wrap around my waist.

I can do this. I can open this bar, commit to a long-distance relationship with Logan without letting it interfere with my job, and be less of a perfectionist. This will be easy.

A throaty moan comes from Logan. Yes, this is going to much easier once we are done making out. Focusing on Logan for just one night isn't going to hurt my career. I can totally handle one night.

CHAPTER FOUR

Logan

"Everyone, we have a new student today."

Mrs. Hills introduces me to my new seventh grade class. She's a tall woman, probably in her mid-thirties with dark brown hair. Her smile is big, warm, and inviting as she gestures with her hand for me to join her at the front of the room. I hate being the center of attention. I hate being noticed.

I stand next to her, near a wooden desk. It looks just like the ones I've seen in movies. It even has that stupid white sticker with a red apple on it that reads "Best Teacher."

"Everyone, say hello to Logan Parker."

I gaze down at the floor, avoiding eye contact with the entire class. Being the new kid is hard, but it's even harder when you're the new kid because you had to switch foster parents due to the fact your last ones didn't want you. I was that kid.

"Logan, don't be shy. Everyone is excited to have you."

I feel her hand touch my shoulder. When I finally move my eyes to her, she's giving me another warm look, her eyes saying, "Don't be scared."

If only she knew scared was something I didn't feel anymore. What was there to be scared of when no one wanted you? If they didn't want you, they couldn't hurt you.

I sigh and look out into the room. Only one kid is paying attention to the teacher. I notice her because her bright blonde hair stands out and she's smiling at me. It's a real smile.

I feel my lips twitch, wanting to smile back, but the sound of Mrs. Hills' voice again reminds me where I am.

"Who wants to show Logan around the school?"

The blonde's hand darts into the air from the back row as something inside me skips. She stands quickly, making her way to the front of the room. I keep staring at her, curious who she is and why, after the past few years of not wanting to know anyone, I want to know her.

"Just be back by the end of the class period," Mrs. Hills says to us.

The blonde nods and turns for the door. I follow her out of the room, stopping next to her when the door closes.

"I'm Sara Connelly," she says, offering her hand to me like an adult.

"Logan Parker."

"I know." She giggles and a blush sweeps over her face. "Mrs. Hills just told us that."

She immediately starts to tell me about the school I'll now be attending. I follow her through the halls, listening to her talk but not exactly paying attention.

Something about her makes me think that this time I'll do

anything it takes to keep my foster family. Anything that keeps me near Sara Connelly.

* * *

I didn't sleep much last night and when I did, it included a brief dream of the day I met Sara. That dream was all I needed to tell me what I already knew.

We were brought together for a reason. I may have been just a kid when I met her, but we've grown up together and learned together. The person she has grown into is a woman I respect and admire. She's always wanted to own her own bar, not just manage the way she does at the BA. I want to be there for her, but I also can't stand in her way. We can make this work. Hundreds of miles between us won't ruin anything. If anything, it might help us.

I have a sister out there somewhere who I might never meet, and not long ago I pushed my friends, Sara included, away because I was having a hard time dealing with it. I told her it was because I was leaving for college and having a girl-friend didn't sound ideal. That was a lie. The fact no one could give me information on my sister is what made my decision. Sara didn't deserve a guy like me. A guy with no family or direction. But things are different now. My friends are my family and this opportunity is setting me in a great direction.

I'd put off finding my sister after high school, but a few months ago, Tyler hacked into the child services computer and got me her address. I sent her a letter. Then, I sent another. Every letter but the first has been returned to me unopened. It feels like a punch in the gut every time I find it in the mailbox, but I'm not giving up. With Sara moving, I might have more time to focus on tracking down my sister without neglecting Sara

Still to this day, I've never told Sara about trying to contact my sister. She doesn't need to be bothered with those kinds of problems. I almost cracked and told her last night, but I only wanted to focus on us, and it wasn't the right time to bring it up. Thinking clearly this morning, I should have told her the truth—if we're going to do this, we can't have any secrets.

I step through the doors into the BA and my phone chirps, notifying me of an incoming call. Mr. Connelly's name flashes across the screen. He called first thing this morning, asking me to meet him here so we could go over a few things. I can't imagine what he could tell me that I don't already know about this place. At eight in the morning no less. It's also a shock that he's actively doing something with the BA other than an approval here or a signature there. He hasn't taken a part since the day he made Sara manager.

"Logan, perfect timing, I was just calling you," Sara's father greets me as I stand frozen in the doorway. Now I see who Sara gets her punctuality from.

"Mr. Connelly." I nod, walking toward him.

"Please, call me Dean," he says, offering me his hand.

I've known this man for more than a decade and never has he invited me to call him by his first name. Sara might not see it, but another reason I'm taking her father's offer is for her. Not only will the money be good, but the closer I am with her father, the better our relationship will be.

"Dean," I say with confidence and shake his hand. I

follow him to the front window and take the seat across from him at one of the high-top tables.

"So, I'll just get right to the point. Ethan spent part of his time as manager searching for local bands. It was an idea he ran by Sara without telling the rest of the bar just in case it fell through. Good news is, we will have live entertainment in this place again. Thanks to Ethan's contacts, I've scheduled a few bands to rotate each Saturday for the next couple of months until we can find more."

I already knew about the bands, but I let him continue. He hands me some flyers that advertise the entertainment: Black Cross, Rowdy Roughhousers, and Mugged. I haven't heard of any of these, and since I'm judging the names, they all sound a bit—harsh.

"This sounds like a great idea. Who, ahh … who picked them?" I ask.

"I did, from a list Ethan provided."

I glance back at the posters. This one flyer must have used all the black ink. *Did he do any research on them?* Sara is going to freak when she finds out her dad may have hired a few hardcore bands to play at the BA. But if the music is good, it won't matter.

"I would like for you to be here on the nights they play, of course. To keep the locals in check."

I keep my eyes focused on the flyer. It's one thing to tell Sara I'm happy leaving the bar under someone else's supervision for a night, but her father might not be as accepting to the idea. If the bands play every Saturday night, that would mean I have to be here every weekend no matter what I told Sara last night. I'll just have to change visits from the weekend to during the week. I look up to see a satisfied grin resting on Dean's lips as he looks over the checklist in front of him.

Did he plan this on purpose?

I shake the idea, because who would do that to their daughter, and nod my head.

"Yeah, I can do that. I may need to switch a few gig nights to Fridays, but it should work," I say. My phone buzzes in my pocket and I resist the urge to check it in front of him.

"I've already arranged for Saturdays, but when the next eight weeks of rotations are done, Fridays will be fine."

Fuck. *Eight weeks.*

"The first band plays this Saturday. That gives you three days to do some extra advertising."

Advertising in three days—he can't be serious.

"The stage needs a few repairs and I think we need to put some new lights above it as well."

The stage looks in perfect condition to me.

"Storage room B needs to be cleared and joined with Storage room A"—he checks something off on the paper in front of him—"the band members will need a place to relax before and after their sets. You will need to buy furniture for that room, and it might be a good idea to put the poster of each band who plays here up in that room as well."

"May I?" I reach for the notepad in front of him as he pushes it toward me. I skim over it quickly. *This is quite the list.*

"Sara and I will be leaving in the morning. I hope we can cross off most of these tasks today."

Tomorrow morning. This confirms it. He's trying to keep me away from his daughter. And that gives me less than twenty-four hours to spend with her before she leaves.

"Logan, Dad, what a surprise to see you here."

Sara's voice relaxes me immediately. I turn and try my best to hide any laughter that tries to escape. There's no hiding the fact she ran here, a perk of living downtown near the bar. And by the sight of her pink slippers, I think she did it in her pajamas too. She's wearing a black pair of too short shorts and a red tank top with her hair looking like a ratted mess on the top of her head. *Damn, she looks sexy.*

Her eyes sparkle when she looks at me and when she blushes, I think she just realized she didn't get ready. Her hands move quickly, smoothing down her clothes and fidgeting with her hair.

"You look—"

"Is everything okay, dear?" her father cuts me off and rushes to her. "I left you a voicemail where I would be. You look like you ran out for an emergency."

Sara rolls her eyes at me, doing her best to hide her smile.

"Well, isn't it? Your voicemail said I'm leaving tomorrow, so the short notice has to mean there's something wrong."

Dean chuckles and takes his seat again.

She can't leave tomorrow. I know my facial expression is cool and calm right now, but inside, I'm freaking out just a little. I just got Sara back from a trip a few weeks ago. A trip I still have no idea why it was so important she take—she hasn't told me much about it. Then again, I haven't asked. We haven't been alone long enough to talk about it.

"I'm sorry to alarm you, dear, but no. I just wanted to get a head start on getting this place up and running. The sooner you get there and get started, the sooner I can make that happen. Now, why don't you go home, pack, and possibly shower? Logan and I have a full day today." He clears his throat and pins his daughter with a "don't argue with me" stare. "We can't have any distractions."

Sara

I glance at my phone, again. It's been two minutes since the last time I checked. When my dad said they would be busy all day, he wasn't joking. I texted Logan the moment I left and it's been a solid nine hours with no response. I wasn't in my right mind last night, and by giving all my attention to Logan, I'm behind on making a checklist of everything I need to do at this new bar before I get there. Checklists make everything easier.

I stare at the blank paper. There is nothing written down because I've spent most of the day concerned over whether or not I'm going to see Logan before I go, and the only conclusion I've come to is that this is the longest day ever.

My other distraction: watching re-runs of *Drop Dead Diva* until my motivation to be successful returns in full force. I hit the power button on the remote before pacing in front of my couch. I hate this unsettling feeling in my gut. Like if I don't see him before I go, I won't see him ever again.

It almost reminds me of the summer before our freshman year. I was so paranoid that Logan and I would end up in different high schools. Wind Valley isn't a very big town, but they still have your typical two rival high schools. Junior high was great for me, but I had a weird vibe that if I didn't have Logan as my study partner for the next four years, my life wouldn't feel right.

At that time, I'd only known part of his background, and I looked up to the way he pushed himself and always remained happy. I thought life was rough as a teenage girl, but life was easy compared to what Logan had been through. So when I walked through the doorway to social studies that first day and found him sitting in the room by himself, that was the moment I knew Logan would forever be important to me. And the way he smiled when he me saw that day, I knew he felt the same way.

"Knock, knock," Kelsey says as she opens the door to my apartment. We used to live here together, but that changed after my cousin Ethan came to town. Now she lives on the other side of Wind Valley and I live alone. Some days it has its perks, but days like today, I'm thankful she's stopped by to keep my mind distracted.

Kelsey pokes her head around the kitchen corner, and I sigh in relief that she's alone. Don't get me wrong, I love my cousin, Ethan, and I love that bundle of joy, Clara. But I miss having my best friend to myself, and right now is the perfect moment to make up for lost time. I let my body fall back into the couch and, with a small bounce, I whine, resting my head against the back cushion.

"Why do I feel frustrated?" I complain. "Owning a bar has been my goal for as long as I can remember, and out of nowhere, leaving feels—different. I'm still excited, just not as excited as I thought I was would be."

"I know. I wish there was something I could say to make you feel better," she says, placing her purse on the kitchen counter and joining me in the living room. Her hair is pulled up into a messy bun, brown strands falling around her face, and she doesn't have makeup on. She's wearing jeans and a plain, black t-shirt that has a smudge of some sort at the bottom—probably a gift from Clara. "You're going to hate this," she says, redirecting my attention back to our conversation. "But you know it's not the end of the world. You just have to go down there, kick ass, and get your butt home as soon as you can."

She takes a seat next to me and pats my leg. I know she's right, but it seems the idea of Logan and me always stirs this terrifying feeling inside me. A glare from the diamond on her ring finger shines on the TV, and instantly I feel a sting in my heart. What if I never get there with Logan? I mean, it's way too early to think about that, but you don't date someone if you don't think marriage could be in your future. What if this changes everything for us?

"I see you're wearing your ring today. Does that mean you two finally told the rest of the world you've been married for a month?" I ask.

My vison begins to grow blurry from stubborn tears so I look out the window, away from her. This right here, my emotional side, this is exactly why I don't do relationships. I'm sitting here worried about Logan and me when I should be making this damn list I've yet to start.

Kelsey rests her hand on my arm and waits until I face her again before she says anything. "This is just another bump in the road, and I know you can handle it."

I sigh heavily and close my eyes.

"My dad has been working him all day. So much that Logan hasn't been able to even text me back. Is this a sign my father doesn't like him?"

"Hey, stop. Your father loves Logan. You dad's even having him run the bar while you're gone. That's *huge*. He would never ask someone he didn't trust."

Again, I know she's right, but there's this little voice in the back of my head telling me my father did this to keep us apart. He's the one who has always taught me how relationships ruin everything. Maybe he's testing me. I push it away before I get too carried away on the idea. My father wouldn't do that me.

"So, tell me what you have planned so far. Do you have appointments set up or anything?"

"A few. An electrician is coming on Tuesday, the painters and tile guys are coming on Wednesday—"

"Nothing like jumping right in." She laughs. "What does that give you, twenty-four hours to settle in and relax?"

I quickly jot the two things on my list before I forget. *There, now I have something written down.*

"Yep. Except my father found me a fully furnished condo a couple blocks away from the new bar. All I have to do when I get there is sign the papers and hang up some clothes," I say, staring at the blank TV screen. He's had the whole thing planned for a while now. I can't believe I never caught on to the fact he was going to give the bar to me. It actually pisses me off a little because we've always done everything as a team.

"Wow, you're really not excited. Your voice has been flat since the moment I walked through that door. I thought I was going to have to take you off cloud nine, since this is what you've wanted since we graduated high school." Kelsey wraps her arms around me and I hug her back. "Don't take this the wrong way, but I find it really cute you're actually flustered over a guy."

I don't want to be flustered. I'm not a fan of surprises. I like knowing what is going to happen.

Kelsey laughs, giving me a side hug as my phone pings in my hand.

Logan: You, me, tonight?
Me: Yes!

First thing tomorrow, I will make a list of what I need to do at the new bar. Tonight it's going to be just me and Logan. Just one more night without thinking of work won't hurt me. But just in case, I better write down a few more things before he gets here.

Number one, finish this list.

CHAPTER FIVE

Logan

No matter what it takes, Sara and I are meant to be together and we will be. I'm not going to let her father get in our way. I know he deliberately kept me at work until almost midnight on our last night together, but his plan failed. The only thing keeping us apart now is my dumb ass. I haven't moved to get out of my truck.

I watch as her bedroom light flicks on and off through her window. She's probably running in and out, checking to make sure she looks just right. I texted her a half hour ago to ask if I could pick her up, even if it's late. She texted "yes" right back, and I know she's most likely been doing whatever she does to make herself look beautiful. I just wish she knew she didn't have to do any of it. She's beautiful no matter how hard she tries. Inside and out. That's why she deserves better than me, but my selfish ass won't let her go. I'll spend the rest of my life proving to her that I am good enough.

I let out a deep breath, open the truck door, and finally get out. I look up to see her standing in the window of her second-floor apartment. She smiles and waves to me before disappearing. I only make it up one flight of stairs before she meets me. With her hair pulled to the side, a sweater that hangs off one shoulder and some black leggings, she looks incredible. Then she blushes and my heart starts to pound faster. I'm one lucky guy.

"Are you going to stand there all night, or are you going to kiss me? You won't get to anytime you want anymore, so you better do it as much as you can tonight," she says. Her smile falters just a bit, but I know she's trying her hardest to stay positive. Still, she's right. I don't want to waste any time. There's nothing gentle about the way my lips crash against hers. Her mouth opens instantly and I slide my tongue inside.

When the main door opens and voices fill the stairwell, we pull apart. Without saying a word I place her hand in mine and guide her down the stairs behind me. I open the passenger door for her to get in and then jog around to my side. The truck roars to life and I head down Main Street.

I turn on the radio to a low volume, but neither of us speaks a word. This is another thing I love about Sara. She doesn't always have to be doing something or talking when we're together. Being together is enough for her and it's more than enough for me.

I turn on Wind River Road and Sara beams at me from her side. I want to be alone with her tonight, and outside under the stars far away from town is the perfect place to be.

I pull up near the meadow where our senior class used to hold parties, the same meadow where we had our first kiss, and my body relaxes. Luck is on my side because the entire place is deserted.

I park the truck and walk around to open her door. She jumps out and places another kiss on my mouth. Her hands wrap around my waist as she pulls me into her. It takes everything I have to stop her. Our physical attraction is equally intense as our mental one.

"Let me get the tailgate down and lay out some blankets. Then we can pick up where we left off."

Nodding her head quickly, Sara opens the back door to my truck and grabs all the blankets I brought with me. This isn't the first time we've been out here, and by this point, we have a routine. I grab the pillows and then flip the tailgate down. Sara climbs up quickly, laying out every blanket and stacking the pillows just the way we like them. She isn't wasting any time.

"I have one more thing," I tell her and disappear into the truck. I grab the flowers I brought with me and return to the back where I find Sara resting back on her elbows.

"Oh, Logan, those are beautiful." She smiles, taking the flowers from my hand and lying them not to her so I can climb up beside her. I bunch the pillows up at the back of the truck and pull her into my arms. With a kiss to the top of her head, she relaxes into my chest.

"Why can't life be like this? Relaxing, happy ... carefree," she says almost whispering.

"Because if life were all those things, we would take them for granted. We want those things because we have to work hard to earn them."

Her arms lay over my stomach and she squeezes me. When Sara leans her head back, I take this moment to pick up where we left off. It's not that I don't want to talk to her, because I do. But right now, I want to feel normal. Like a guy who finally got the girl and things are perfect. Not the guy who finally got the girl and she's moving.

My lips graze hers, and everything inside my heart says take it slow because even though I will see her again, I don't know when that will be. I told her I'd make the drive to Rockland, but if I'm honest with myself, this position at the bar is going to take a lot of time and effort. I want her to see that I'm dedicated—that I have goals just like her. My mind on the other hand, is screaming to touch every inch of her skin. Yelling for me to make this moment the best I can make it. Tonight's going to be the last memory she has before she leaves, and I have to make it count.

Sara

I find it a little strange that whenever Logan and I get into the perfect make-out session, my back always seems to be rubbing up against something painful. There are exactly six blankets below me and I can still feel the steel of the truck underneath me as I'm underneath Logan. I find it even stranger that I still don't care. I'm loving every minute of it. The way his body feels against mine. The way his hips grind into my body. The way he tastes like wintergreen, smells like fresh cut hardwood, and the sounds he makes when I move with him. A moan from him sets my entire body on fire.

I do, however, care about this damn multitasking brain of mine.

I've never been a relationship kind of girl. Then again, Logan's last official girlfriend was me during high school. But still, balancing the focus between Logan and work is something I already know is going to be difficult. Right now, my mind is screaming "work comes first," but my heart is beating "Logan comes first."

"Hey, beautiful." Logan pulls away and gazes down at me. "I think I lost you there for a second." He forces a half smile, but I can see in his eyes he knows exactly where my mind has been. "It was like kissing a statue. My lips were moving, but yours weren't."

I swallow the lump in my throat and look away. "I'm sorry, I can't help it. You know how my mind works."

"I do." He sighs. "Were you thinking about me or work?"

Logan removes the leg nestled between mine and lies on his hip. Resting on his arms, he keeps his body facing me and leaves his eyes fully focused on mine.

"Both," I answer.

"And what we're you thinking?"

"That I want this bar, but I want you, too, and I'm not sure I'm going to be able to do it."

Another sigh slips past his lips. He's already frustrated with me. Maybe we should just date when I get back at the end of the summer.

"Logan, right now—"

"—is the perfect time to date. Sara, I know you haven't grown up in a family with parents who loved each other, but neither did I. We are Sara and Logan. We are the best when we are together, and we're made for each other. We've never had to date for me to see this." His hand rubs the small of my back.

He's right. We've always been flirty together, and I'm happiest when he's around. That just never occurred to me until I left last summer.

"You know that, I know that, the whole world knows it.

You won't be gone forever, and I will do everything I can to see you when time allows it."

It honestly feels like my heart just grew a little bigger from his words. I want to cry and can already feel the tears sneaking their way out. I take a deep breath and blink them away, but the attempt is gone when Logan releases me from his arms and props one knee up in front of me. He then holds my hand in his.

"Sara Connelly, you are stubborn, driven, brilliant, and beautiful. These are a few of the reasons I want to be in your life. I know you love your career and I know you want this bar. I also know you want to be a part of my life, too. I would never make you choose between either of those things."

"Logan—"

"Wait, I'm not finished." He kisses my forehead. "I, too, want to be successful and I want that with you. I know how hard you've worked, and I promise you I will live up to your expectations at the BA. However, I do have one thing to ask of you."

If your heart could stop and beat a million times in one second, my heart is doing that right now. My hand is shaking in his as I wait for him to continue.

"Will you promise me that no matter how overwhelmed you are, you will call me, text me, anything, before you give up on us? You have to trust that we will work. I want to give this a real chance, but I don't want either of us to give up anything for it. Selfish I know, but—"

"Yes!" I shout without even thinking twice about it. "I can promise you that."

I hug him then and kiss him because I clearly have a lot to learn about relationships and I'm going to learn with Logan.

CHAPTER SIX

Logan

My intentions tonight were to walk her home, since she lives in the building next to mine, and be a gentleman with just a good-night kiss. But Sara has plans of her own and I'm not doing anything to stop her.

She squeals against my lips as I step inside her apartment and close the door. I'll never get over that sound. She slowly drops to her feet, never letting our lips part.

There's no hesitation as Sara's small and delicate fingers tug at my waistband and unbutton my pants. She tugs the zipper quickly, pulling my jeans down just a bit. "I want these off," she says hungrily before meeting my eyes with a fiery blaze in her own. I've never seen her look at me like this. We've had sex before—in high school and once before she left last summer. It was amazing, mind-blowing sex, but something tells me things are about to get even more exciting.

I release a growl of frustration as I grab her hand and pull her toward her bedroom. Somewhere along the way, she kicks off her shoes and lets go of my hand to remove her sweater. *She never was the type to waste time.* I stop her before she can pull it over her head and hold her arms down at her sides. "Don't," I say, and she inhales at the deep tone of my voice. "I want to be the one to remove your clothes."

Her body trembles and goose bumps cover her perfect, soft skin. I let her arms go and she backs up until she reaches the bed. In one step I'm in front of her, pushing her back and letting my body gently land on top of hers. I use my knee to kick her legs apart until I can settle my hips between them. At the contact of our bodies, Sara moans and, if possible, I grow harder in my jeans.

"Stop teasing me, Logan. I want you and I don't want to wait."

She doesn't have to ask me twice. I swiftly remove her shirt, and in seconds our pants are gone too. Placing myself back between her legs, I reach to her nightstand and grab a condom.

"Hurry," she breathes beneath me.

I tear the packet open quickly and roll it onto myself. In one move, I'm inside her. She inhales as I exhale. I move slowly, soaking in this moment and the way she feels around me. Her uneven breathing and a nudge from her heel at the crease of my back makes me move faster. I do exactly as she asks until we both reach that moment of release together.

Sara

Saying goodbye to Logan when I left for Europe was so much easier. We weren't an item then. Yeah sure, we hooked up, which totally freaked me out because I didn't realize I could fall so hard for someone, and then two weeks before I left I thought I was pregnant—something Logan doesn't know. False alarm, of course, but that scare was the last straw to make me run. But right now, I don't feel that way at all.

I can't peel my eyes away from the gorgeous man lying next to me. His soft, tan skin. That blonde hair I used to think was too long, but now, this close up, is perfect. If it's possible for a man to have long, dark lashes, he has the best ones. His bare and toned chest rises as he takes slow, steady breaths, and his lips part slightly. God, I could fall asleep to that face every night and have such sweet, sweet dreams. Hopefully, they would be active ones, but then again, I could just wake him up and make those dreams real.

"Babe, why aren't you sleeping?"

He reaches an arm over and pulls me toward him. When I'm close enough that I could just pucker my lips and kiss him, he opens his eyes. A spark comes from them and I try not to blink as I look back. I'm going to miss him more than I even knew possible. My heart feels like it's being squeezed dry just thinking about it.

"You're beautiful, and I'm crazy lucky to be here with you."

"Hey"—he kisses my forehead—"that's my line."

The smile that tugs at his lips matches exactly how I feel.

God, could he be any cuter?

"You know," I tease, "those are some sexy words, Mr. Parker."

"Indeed they are, Ms. Connelly."

"Well, what—"

"That's enough talking," he says, grabbing my hips and pulling me until I'm sitting on top of him. Not putting our clothes back on is really paying off right now. With a hand on each side of my face, he sits up to kiss me. As he leans back, I go with him, never letting my lips part from his.

* * *

"I should probably get going. It's already five, and your dad would be disappointed if he knew I kept you up all night before you left." Logan reluctantly moves out of bed and starts to pull on his boxers.

I watch but don't say anything.

"Sara, if you keep looking at me like that, I won't be gone anytime time soon."

I love the way he says my name.

"Well … that's okay with me. Maybe I don't want you to go just yet."

Logan tosses his shirt onto the floor and his muscles flex when he leans onto the bed and crawls over me. I start to push the sheets away, letting him know what I want, but he quickly presses his hands down around me, tucking me into the sheet. Once he has me tight enough, he starts to tickle me. I can't move because my arms are pinned under the sheets and he's now sitting on my legs.

"Stop it," I shout between laughs. I try to sit up and twist or turn out of his hands, but he is too strong for me. "Please, please, I'll do anything just stop, stop it, please."

"Anything, huh? I may have to take you up on that offer. But right now, I really should be going." Logan moves off the bed. He's dressed and pulling on his shirt the second I get out bed. I walk straight past him to the bathroom. I'm fully aware I have no clothes on and so is he.

"Sara, I'm warning you. Keep taunting me, and I won't be able to resist you."

"I'm not exactly sure I want you to," I tell him and close the door right before he reaches me. Taking a deep breath, I lean against it. Goodbyes have never been a strong area for me and doing them in a new relationship is definitely out of my comfort zone. I grab my robe and swing the door open. Logan's still standing there.

"I really do need to go." He kisses me long and hard. "Call me when you get there."

I nod, watching him leave.

I'm pretty sure calling him definitely should come before finishing that damn list.

CHAPTER SEVEN

Sara

It's been two weeks and I'm going insane. Logan hasn't had a chance to make good on that plan to take a weekend off. Fortunately, the bands are bringing in more than the usual BA crowd, so Logan has been spending a lot of time hiring more help. I love that Logan is making sure the BA isn't short-handed, but I hate how much of his time it takes up. Phone calls can only go so far. And I especially hate how much the thought of not seeing him is taking up more room in my brain than this bar.

My father is keeping busy, too. His role in this new bar is nice; I haven't seen him lend a hand in years. The new task for me is hiring an assistant manager. He was against it at first, but when he noticed how busy I've been, he came around.

For a while I thought he was seriously losing his mind, expecting me to open this place all on my own. He called me an hour ago and told me I had better get to work *now* because

I have three interviews this morning. *Three.* There aren't even any tables or chairs, except a few barstools, for me to sit at while I conduct these interviews. No artwork or anything on the walls. The paint is still trying to dry. I thought I'd at least have another week or more to get that stuff in here before I started interviewing.

On the plus side, the sooner I hire someone, the easier it is for me to go home this weekend for Kelsey's birthday, and the sooner I go home, for good, the sooner Logan and I can be together.

I pass a coffee shop, an accessory store, and a vintage dress shop on my way to work. All places where I've become a regular customer. I have to hand it to my father, at least he picked a part of town I would enjoy. Having everything I love in a one-block radius is amazing. Only one thing would make this better: Logan.

We talk almost every day and it's great, but seeing each other would be better. I promised him I would be there for Kelsey's party. I feel a bit guilty for already planning to spend most of my weekend with Logan and less time with my father. He has to expect this though, right? I mean, I am growing up and this is what grown women do—we branch off and become our own person.

I pull my phone from my purse to send Logan a quick text. If everything goes as planned, I can leave this Friday by noon. I let out a little giggle, and there's definitely some pep to my step as I type what I think is a flirty message, but before I can hit send, I run into a brick wall. Or at least what I thought was a brick wall. I panic and hit the ground hard with my knees in an attempt to save my phone. I'm too late. My cell hits the cement and the cover breaks away from the phone. The screen is shattered, and no matter how many times I press the power button, it won't turn on.

"Aren't those type of cases supposed to be life-proof or something?" A deep voice says from above me. I don't look up. My main form of contact with anyone is gone. How am I going to talk to Logan now? How am I going to contact my dad, or what number will I give the interviewees? Unless this guy giving me some speech on life-proof cases works for a cell phone company and has a new phone for me, his opinion is the last thing I need.

A hand comes into my view and catches my attention. My eyes travel the length of the toned arm to a huge bicep, and my eyes go wide when I see what's standing in front of me. A black t-shirt hugs a large, solid chest, and dark blue jeans hang just right around a set of hips with a brown belt. A man, who looks to be around my age, with short, black hair and light green eyes studies me. His lips form into a half smile.

"You aren't even going to try to act like you weren't checking me out just now?" he asks as he glances over me. His smile grows wider. "Interesting."

"I—"

Crap. How am I going to explain that one?

"I'm sorry," I finally say once I've stood and brushed myself off. I'm wearing a red dress that flows just above my knees, and now you can see small divots in my knees where tiny bits of gravel have been.

He laughs and then slings a black backpack over his shoulder.

"Actually, I'm glad you were checking me out. I have an interview today, and I think you just gave me all the confidence I need to go in there with my head held high."

"Oh—"

"Sorry about your phone. I was looking for this new bar, but I can't seem to find it. The Silver Tap, have you heard of it?"

I swallow the embarrassing amount of spit that formed in my mouth from watching him. That's my bar; he's interviewing with me. *Crap again.*

"Ummm, yeah—there isn't a sign yet, but it should be up in the next few weeks," I tell him.

"No way, are you Sara? I'm Liam," he says, extending his hand. I give it a firm shake before I respond.

"That's me."

"But, you look so young."

"I am, but not too young that I don't know how to run my own business," I respond with more of an authoritative tone. "Let's move inside. I need to make a phone call before we get started." And sadly, the phone in the office is the only one I have now.

"Yeah, okay. Cool."

Liam follows behind me as we make our way to the bar, and I can feel his eyes on me the entire way. It's … different. Someone once told me that you become more desirable the moment you're off limits. Maybe that person was right after all. *I am pretty damn desirable.* I laugh inwardly at my own joke. Sneaking a peek over my shoulder, I grin when I notice Liam isn't paying any attention to me. Good, can't have him thinking he is about to be working for a crazy lady who laughs at her own mental jokes.

I unlock the door and flip the switch to turn on the lights. This place looks like a spitting image of the BA. The only difference is the platform the entrance is on. In Wind Valley, you step down when you walk in—here, you step up. Everything else, down to the colors inside, are the same. It's been working for the BA, so what's not to say it won't work well here, too?

"Why don't you just pull up a seat at the bar and I'll be out in a minute," I tell him as I walk toward my office. He nods and heads for the bar. I hear his backpack hit the floor and I jump a little. The noise reminding me that I'm in an empty, unopened bar with a total stranger and no cell service.

I close the door behind me as I step into the office and quickly lock it. It's small. Much smaller than the one in Wind Valley, and here the metal desk takes up half the room. Stacks of papers and rolled up posters fill the corners. A few have fallen over. I lean them upright and then let my body fall into the squeaky leather chair behind the desk.

I had argued with my father about having a landline in here. I knew eventually we would need one, but I thought it was silly to want one when the place isn't even open. But now that my cell is shattered, I'm thinking my dad can be pretty smart.

I should call him first, but I dial Logan's number quickly instead and wait as it rings.

A flashback to the first time I ever called Logan makes me smile. I swear he didn't answer that day on purpose just so I'd have to call back. The more I dialed, the more committed I became to winning his attention.

When I get his voicemail my smile fades and I glance at the clock. It's not early. He should be up by now. Did something happen to him? What if he's hurt and no one thought to contact me?

The knocking at the door pulls me from my trance.

"One minute," I call out. I need to pull myself together before this guy runs because his potential new boss is a hot mess. I take a deep breath and unlock the door.

Liam is back sitting at the bar when I come out. His backpack is lying on the seat next to him, and he has a mini bar set up in front of him. I clear my throat and he turns around quickly.

"Hey, so, your father mentioned the place isn't stocked yet and told me if I really want to impress you, I would find a way. So, here it is." He pulls a Vanna White to display everything on the bar top. "As you see here, I have all the ingredients to make you the best Bloody Mary you will ever taste. Vodka, spicy tomato juice, pickles, olives, salt and pepper, a celery stick, and even one of these fun, little, plastic knives to hold it all together."

I press my lips together to hide my smile. This guy has creativity and definitely came prepared. A mind like that could be useful around here.

"I hate to break it to you," I say, pointing to his set up and then to the empty shelves behind him. "But we don't have any glasses for me to try this best Bloody Mary ever."

He smirks and holds up a finger while he reaches for his bag. He then pulls out a single glass and a few other supplies to make the drink.

"Huh." I take a seat at the bar and swing my legs around to face the back wall. I sit up tall and lace my hands together. This should be good. "Okay, go around and pretend I'm a customer. Let's see how your social skills are. I need someone who is a good people person. All employees will need to be capable of working every area in the bar."

"Easy," he says with a cocky grin and moves to the other

side of the bar. "If we're going to make this real, at least pretend you just walked up to the bar. I would never make a customer wait as patiently as you have been," he says with a wink. Hopefully, I get up fast enough before he can see me blush. Between his smile and his smooth winking skills, he will definitely make good tips from the ladies. I take two steps away from my seat, then turn around and walk back to it.

"Hey there, welcome to the Silver Tap. What can I get you to drink this fine afternoon?" He gives me another wink as he uses the flirtiest tone I've ever heard. His smile grows bigger, and I know this time he didn't miss the rosy color in my checks.

"A beer is fine. Thanks," I say calmly. *Ha!* Now who's uncomfortable?

"I hate to break it to you, pretty lady, but I'm fresh out of beer. However, as luck would have it, I have everything needed to make you the best Bloody Mary you've ever tasted."

I don't even get a chance to let him know I don't like vodka before he continues.

"And if you don't like it, it's on me."

His confidence is good but almost comes off as cocky. Men will definitely hate it, and women—well, on second thought, it's going to be hit or miss until they are drunk enough to think he's flirting with only them. And I'll definitely tell him that if he ever buys a drink, it better come from his pocket and not the bar's because that will not work for me. But I'll take the bait.

"Okay, let's see what you can do, oh grand bartender."

"Perfect!" He claps his hands together and gets to work

making my drink. "So, what brings you to Colorado?" he asks while never taking his eyes off what his hands are doing.

"Oh, it's a long story," I say, waving my hand in the air. *Did we put fans in here?*

"I've got time," he says, still not looking up at me. Man, he is really focused. I watch him for a moment, but he doesn't say anything. He seems nice enough, and I haven't really had a moment to vent since I got here. As long as his paperwork checks out, I'll probably end up hiring him since it sounds like he has already been introduced to my father, and he did go through all this trouble to impress me.

"Well, my dad bought me this place as a birthday gift. So, here I am, leaving everything and everyone behind to come open up the place." I let out a long sigh. "Which shouldn't bother me, except it does and that annoys me. I should be happy, right, that my father is helping me move forward? I shouldn't be sitting here wondering what anyone else is doing or who they're hanging out with while I'm in an entirely different state. Which then leads me to the question of whether or not I should be making friends while I'm here. I'm distracted enough by the idea of Logan that adding a friend might add to the focus I already don't have."

A quick glance tells me I've rambled so much that Liam has finished making my drink and is now looking at me with confusion.

"So," he starts, "we're not still in the role of bartender and customer?"

Crap.

"Oh—"

To keep myself from saying anything else, I grab the Bloody Mary in front of me and quickly begin drinking, ignoring the straw. One gulp. Two. *This is good.* Three gulps.

"Whoa, whoa! These are some sneaky drinks. You don't want to be drunk all day, do you?" Liam asks as he takes the drink from my hands. Concern etched in his eyes.

That's not a bad idea. It has been almost a year since I've been drunk. It's not something I enjoy doing, but it happens.

"I don't think I'll have to interview anyone else. You're hired," I say quickly and dart once again for my office. "Be here tomorrow at ten in the morning."

I give him a half-assed wave goodbye because I'm too embarrassed to face him, and hide in my office until he's gone. I need to call Dad ASAP to find out how exactly he found Liam. If he was that intent on Liam impressing me, he clearly knows this guy knows what he is doing.

I pick up the landline and instantly dial Logan, again. This is one of those situations when he told me to call him, and talking to him might actually help me concentrate. The trick now is whether or not he answers.

Logan

"Abby, can you answer that for me?" I call out as my phone rings from across the room. It's been ringing nonstop all day. After the first few calls weren't from Sara, I gave up expecting her to call me until later tonight. Until then, I'm in the middle of inventory and would like to get it done today.

Turns out, no one wants to come to work early on a Monday because it doesn't include tips. As the new manager I should just assign employees to come in, but everything still feels awkward, and I'm having a hard time telling my friends what to do. Lucky for me, Abby and Beth both volunteered. I'll have to ask Sara how she handles being a friend and a boss when she comes home next weekend.

My phone continues to ring, and I stand from my spot behind the bar to see where Abby ran off to. I'm a little thrown to find her standing in front of my phone just looking at it.

"You want to answer that?" I ask again.

"Oh, uh—" She looks at me quickly before she taps the screen, cutting off the ringtone. "It was an unknown caller. I wasn't sure if I should or not." She gives my phone a little push away from her. Her arms swing at her sides as she heads in my direction.

Abby is trouble. I've known this all my life, but for some reason, we keep her around. Somewhere down inside—deep, *deep* down inside—she's a good person. But lately not so much and right now as she steps closer with a flirtatious smile on her face, I know she's up to something. That spark in her eyes is another dead giveaway.

"So, when was last time you talked to Sara?" she asks, tapping her fingers on a table as she passes it.

Oh yeah. The tone in her voice definitely confirms she's setting me up for something not good. Whatever she has planned isn't going to work well in her favor. Damn, hasn't she figured out that we all grew up together and that we know her better than she thinks?

"I appreciate your concern, Abby, but right now, we need to get this inventory done." I use my best strict management voice. "And I'm pretty sure you asking about my personal life crosses a line now that I'm your manager."

I flip the top paper on my clipboard back as I shake my

head and look at the list of items we still need to account for. Between Abby and inventory, this day is more challenging than I want it to be. If Sara would call, it would definitely help me take away some stress.

Abby shuffles her feet in front of me, and when I look up she pushes her bottom lip out and gives me a sad look. Then she lets out the most exaggerated sigh I've ever heard.

"You're no fun anymore. I don't like the person Sara has turned you into. You used to love talking about other people."

"First of all, I never like to talk about people when they aren't around. You must have me confused with someone else, and second, I'm still the same person I was yesterday or six months ago, and finally, Sara hasn't done anything to change me. How could she? She isn't even here."

Her smile is back.

Damn. She was looking for information, probably to find a weakness of mine, and I just gave her exactly she wanted.

This girl is sneaky.

"I think you need someone who would pick you over their job, Logan. You deserve someone who wants to treat you better then you are obviously being treated and not turn you into one of her father's little soldiers just like her. A girl who wants to be with you every—"

"Oh, give it up, Abby. If you cared even an ounce for someone other than yourself for sixty seconds, you would see that Logan and Sara do nothing but bring out the best in each other." Beth rolls her eyes as she comes out of the back room and sets a box of Bud bottles on the bar top. "What's next, Logan? We better get a move on since it looks like we're the only ones who came here today to actually work," she says, cocking her head and glaring at Abby. "Unless, of course,

Abby, you're done trying to ruin another relationship between some of our friends. Oh wait, no that's right—*my* friends. Because if they were your friends, too, you wouldn't be pestering Logan right now about Sara."

And this is exactly why I need to hire more men in this place. *Drama.* Now that Ethan is gone and Lucas, another bartender, is in Florida for three weeks, I'm the only one left.

"Okay, let's all just get to work," I say before this can get out of control. "We are really off topic right now, and Beth is right. I want this done before we open."

Abby releases another sigh that screams for attention and when no one says anything, she narrows her eyes at me. *Typical.* I'm the only guy so this is my fault.

"Fine, what do you want me to do?" she asks with her hands on her hips.

"Why don't you go do some work in the storage room, away from Logan?" Beth says, wasting no time.

Fuck. I have to get some control over this place.

Abby glances back and forth between us, glaring at Beth. I tilt my head toward the storage room in agreement.

"Let's just get this day over with without any more drama," I say to her and then glance at Beth as well. I didn't forget the one rule Sara emphasized: Never make direct eye contact when making a rule or statement that applies to every-one. The person you're looking at will always take it person-ally if you do.

With her arms crossed, Abby finally storms off. My head falls back as I close my eyes.

"You've really got to get a handle on being the boss, Logan. That girl takes extra work, and if you don't man up soon, she will walk all over you."

I groan to myself. "I know, I know. I wish there were more guys in this town who wanted a bar job."

"It's easier for girls to make tips off drunk men than it is for men to make tips off drunk women."

I nod. "Again, I know."

"But I heard the other day when I was having lunch with Kelsey that her brother is in town. I'm not sure if he is staying for a while or not, but even temporary man help is good, right?"

Conner Brian, Kelsey's brother. He's perfect. I've always liked that guy. We get along great, and he doesn't take shit from anyone. They only downfall: he's single.

"One problem," I say holding up a finger. Switching from my index finger to my thumb, I point to the storage room. "That girl senses a single man ten miles away and pounces."

Beth laughs. "Better him than you, right?"

I consider it for a moment, and when I hear a crash from the storage room, my decision is made. "I guess it won't hurt anything," I tell Beth as she disappears to join Abby in the back. My phone rings again and this time I choose to answer it. I make my way to the table where I left it and pick it up mid-ring.

"Hello?"

"Logan, it's Dean."

"Mr. Connelly, it's great to hear from you. I hate to sound rude, but is everything okay?" It's not common for Mr. Connelly to call my cell.

"Oh yes, Logan, everything is fine. I was just calling to inform you that Sara has broken her phone and probably won't be able to be reached until later today when she has time to get a new one."

Weird. Why wouldn't she just call me? I know she has my number and the BA's memorized.

"Oh, alright. Well, thank you for calling."

"Of course, Sara asked that I call you since you haven't been answering your phone."

When did she call me?

"Logan, we need help!" Beth calls from the back room.

"Well, there you have it. It sounds like you're busy. I'll be sure to let my daughter know. Have a lovely afternoon, Logan."

Before I can clear up the assumption in his voice, the line goes dead. When did Sara call? And what number did she call me from? And why didn't I … fuck. I quickly scroll through my contacts, but other than Dean's number, I have no unknown numbers in my phone. Damn it, Abby!

I take a long deep breath before I head for the storage room. That girl needs to cut this shit out. As for me, what am I supposed to do? Do I really accuse her of being that crazy? I need to hire another guy in the next twenty-four hours. I tap a text to Ethan and ask for Conner's number before shoving the phone into my pocket, then open the storage door to find an entire case of beer bottles shattered on the floor.

Fuck.

CHAPTER EIGHT

Sara

The next few days drag on like they're never going to end. Liam is learning fast and some of the stress of getting this place ready is being lifted. Since I couldn't get ahold of Logan, I girled up and called my father to ask how he and Liam knew each other.

He met Liam a few months back when he was searching for new buildings during a trip to Colorado. A friend of my father's invited him to speak during one of his business administration classes at the university. Liam was in this class and, apparently, my father saw "great" potential in him right away.

He wasn't entirely wrong. Liam has been nothing but "great" since he started, but every day that I see him, I wish he were Logan. They say absence makes the heart grow fonder. Well, not only does it do that, but it scares the shit out of me too. A lot can happen when two people are apart for too long.

"So, do you want all high-top tables?" Liam asks, the sudden sound of his voice causing me to jump. "Or just some around the outside of the floor with short tables in the center or vice versa? I mean, I guess we could do all regular tables." For the last hour he has been sitting at the bar, browsing on the computer for someone we can purchase tables from. There was an issue with our original contact, who said he wouldn't be able to get the tables we want delivered by the day I want. A delay is not in my plans.

Tapping the pen I've been using to mark up a liquor order against my temple, I glance over at him. He runs his hand through his hair and lets it fall to his lap. *Logan does that.* Liam has on another pair of dark wash jeans and a red tee shirt. If I weren't so crazy about Logan, I would probably have fallen for Liam's dark and mysterious appeal by now. After all, I never thought a guy could remind me so much of Logan, but Liam acts just like him.

"I think mixing it up would make the most sense. Don't you?" I ask, setting the pen down and crossing my arms. "I mean, we're mostly a bar, not a restaurant, and the BA has mostly high-top tables. I want people to know these bars are connected. We better stick with it."

Liam's eyes search my face and he nods his head.

"You seem a little out of it today. Is everything alright?" he asks, and I'm a little taken back at how sincere his voice is. It's only been a few days. How can he already tell when something isn't right?

I shake my head and force a smile. "Everything is fine." I pick up my pen and focus on the liquor order.

"You want to talk about it?"

I shake my head again. "I promise, everything is fine."

"Okay, well, look I'm aware that you've had to leave all your friends and family behind. I mean you and that Logan guy clearly have a thing going on, and Dean said you were finally giving it a go when he sent you down here."

They talked about me. About my love life. My father barely knows this guy. And how in the world are they already on a first-name basis?

"Why would my father talk to you about me?"

Liam pauses with his mouth open. His bottom lip twitches as though he is about to say more, but he closes his mouth and frowns.

"I just want you to know that I have pretty great listening skills. And if it's about a guy, I think I could give some pretty great advice. I know a lot about them."

He stands up, pulling his jacket off the bar, and heads for the door.

"I've got some things to do on the east side of town near a few furniture warehouses. I'll pop in and see what they have in stock for tables, alright? I'll be back in a bit."

He doesn't even wait for my reaction before he steps through the door.

I can't tell if I'm upset my father talks to him about me, confused he seems to really care, or angry. I'm angry because his departure made me notice how not together this place is and how the chances of being done by the end of summer are fading fast. I'm also a bit thrown off at the fact he just left. I should probably put him on a schedule.

The phone rings behind the office door and I almost sprint to it in hopes that it's Logan.

"Hello?" I sound a bit out of breath.

"Sara, how are things going there? Everything moving

along smoothly?" My father's voice does nothing but add to the depressing stupor I've fallen into in the last five minutes.

"Hi, Dad. Yeah, everything is going fine."

"Liam is working out well?"

"Yeah, he's a great help. Hey, should we hire someone else in addition to Liam? I don't think this place is going to be up and running as soon as we want with just Liam and me. It might make sense to get employees in here sooner rather than later. Oh, and how did you come onto the subject of me and Logan with him?"

Silence.

"Dad?"

"Sorry, dear, the phone cut out. Listen, I can't chat long, but I wanted to let you know it would be a great opportunity for Liam to learn more if he came home with you this weekend."

Now it's my turn to be silent. He can't be serious. I haven't seen Logan in weeks and now my father wants me to show up with another guy I've known less than a week?

"We can have him train at the BA over the weekend."

Oh right. This is work related.

"He could stay in your spare room if it's available."

"It's not," I blurt out. What the heck is my dad thinking? Liam is still kind of a stranger. "Sorry, I—told a friend she could crash there while I was home." I let out a breath. "I'll talk to Liam when he gets back and see if he is available. It's a little short notice."

"I spoke with him this morning. He's very well aware and was pleased by my invite."

I roll my eyes. Sometimes I think my father considers

himself some form of royalty. Every time we talk, I swear his words sound more and more formal.

"Dad, you gave me this bar, so I should be the one to make these sort of calls, don't you think?"

"Until the papers are finalized with your name as owner, I'll make the calls."

"And when are those papers coming in, Dad? You told me they would be here this week and I took your word for it."

"Soon, dear. Now, I have to go, but we can finish discussing this when you come home this weekend."

He ends the call before I can reply. Shaking the conversation from my head, I review the list in front of me, looking for the next item on my to-do list. Keeping busy keeps my mind from overthinking, and making a final read-through on the alcohol contract sounds like a great distraction.

Logan

Every computer cubicle in Wind Valley's High School library is filled, each student working quietly. And although the room is silent, my mind is loud with the anticipation of how Sara will reply when I ask her out today.

Tyler's girlfriend, Kelsey—who also happens to be Sara's best friend—well, she told Tyler that Sara is into me. Like really into me. Not just as a friend the way I thought she saw me. And ever since he shared this piece of information, I've been going crazy deciding how I'm going to ask her out.

"Logan," Sara whispers next to me. My neck pops as I turn to look at her. I painfully rub it while she looks at me with sympathy. After a moment, she slips a piece of paper into my work area. I glance around to be sure Mr. Cleo, the librarian,

isn't watching us. When I find him comfortably sitting at his desk with his head down, I quickly unfold the note.

Do you feel okay? You look like you're sweating and you're a bit pale.

I scribble something to tell her I'm just fine and pass the note back to her. It's embarrassing how obvious I am. The note comes back fast.

You promise you would tell me the truth?

Again, I scribble that of course I would tell her, she's my best friend. Before I can think too hard about the fact I wrote the word friend, fully ruining my chance, her hand touches mine and she leans into me.

"You really just want to be my friend, Logan?" she asks, her words so soft and quiet I know for a fact no one heard them but me. Instead of answering, I take a deep breath and press my lips against hers.

"Hey, you two!"

We both jump at Mr. C's voice.

"Get back to your work, and I don't want to see that again."

Facing forward in my seat, I pull out a fresh piece of paper. As clearly as I can in my handwriting, I write my reply.

• • •

I will never just be your friend, Sara.

And from that day forward, I never was.

* * *

"Dude, how many times have you changed your shirt?" Ethan asks sarcastically, pulling me off of memory lane.

"As many times as I need to. I want to look good for Sara."

She comes home today and I'm going to surprise her with a picnic dinner and a movie night in the park with a little dancing after. Technically, it's our first official date as a couple again, and I'm not going to screw this up. I'm planning to make the entire two days I have with her the best. I miss her, and I'm not afraid to show it.

"She has seen everything you own a million times, man. Whatever you pick will be fine. Sara isn't a material kind of person—you do know that, right?" His brows come to a point as he looks at me with pity.

"Yeah, man, I do know that." Doesn't mean I can't look nice.

I flip the collar of my navy-blue polo down and give myself a dab of men's Lucky You cologne.

"You sure it's cool if Conner crashes here for a while?" Ethan takes a seat on my couch, making himself comfortable as he waits for Conner's arrival to check the place out. He crosses his ankle over his knee and leans back as he grabs the motorcycle magazine stuffed between the cushions.

"Definitely," I say. I have a plan to turn my lease over to

Conner when Sara's back so we can get a place together. It may sound like I'm rushing it, but this is Sara. I have faith in us.

I grab my wallet off the counter and slip on my watch. My cell phone buzzes in my pocket as I start for the door.

Sara: Finally got a new phone! Can't wait to see you.
Me: Me too

There is a spring in my step as I hop in my truck and drive to a flower shop a few blocks over. Arranging the schedule to give myself a Friday night off felt weird. I feel bad for being so selfish, but when I think about who I'm going to spend the night with, any guilt is gone.

With lilies in hand, I shoot a text to Sara, letting her know I'm on my way. Then I shoot another text to my buddy Tyler. Except he hasn't really been my buddy since he cheated on Kelsey, but that's all in the past. Since my letters keep coming back, I need him to find out if my sister's mailing address has changed for some reason. If you're going to have a friend who's genius smart, pick the one who can hack almost anything. Tyler is that friend for me.

Once I hit send, I turn the key and head for Sara's. I've got a plan to find my sister, and my girlfriend waiting for me. Life couldn't be better.

CHAPTER NINE

Sara

Tears sting my eyes as I watch Logan walk up the stairwell to my apartment with the largest arrangement of lilies I've ever seen. He smiles at me, and we just stare at each other. In this moment, we don't need to say anything because we already know how the other feels. I never thought I would be so excited to see someone, but I'm slowly learning that everything is different with Logan. Then, our moment is ruined.

"Ok, so I'll call you tomorrow then. Or you're coming over for breakfast, that's right. Sorry, I keep forgetting. That car ride was killer. This state is nothing but dead grass and hills. How your dad managed to talk me into this, I have no idea. I still can't believe he offered to let me stay—"

My eyes pleading for Liam to stop talking finally do their job. Liam drops his bag and extends his hand toward Logan.

"Hey, man, you must be Logan. I've heard so much about you. The name's Liam."

Logan's eyes narrow as he looks at Liam's hand. The coldness doesn't leave them when he glances at me. I swallow the lump in my throat. I've never seen Logan go from happy to mad so quickly.

"Funny, man, cuz I've heard nothing about you."

My eyes go wide at the tone of Logan's voice. I've never heard that voice before either. It sounds so deep. Powerful. Masculine. Logan has never looked so sexy! *Poor Liam.* You could almost hear him gulp as he shook Logan's hand. I definitely didn't miss the tense bob of his throat as he did it.

"Okay, well, Liam, you should get going. We have plans," I say quietly as I gesture to Logan. I give Liam a friendly and hopefully gentle push away from my door.

"Oh right, damn, man, sorry I ruined that there for a sec. I'm gone." He raises his hands like he's surrendering as he backs up toward the stairs. "Act like I wasn't even here."

I laugh as he jumps down the steps two at a time and then I glance at Logan. There's nothing left to laugh about. Now it's me who you hear take a scared swallow at the stare Logan is giving me.

"Anything you want to tell me?"

I shake my head. "That's the new assistant manager in Colorado. I guess, according to my dad, you'll be training him this weekend." I shrug and relax as Logan's angry expression lightens and quickly turns to one that suggests he was afraid.

"So you work with him, every day?"

"For now, yes. Eventually, I'll be able to let him do things on his own. After this weekend with you, I'm hoping that will be sooner rather than later." I quickly put the flowers in some water before grabbing my green jean jacket off the hook behind my door and joining Logan in the hallway. Once the door is locked, I push onto the tips of my toes to give Logan the kiss he should have had the moment he arrived.

"Oh, uh—"

Seriously!

Does this guy have bad timing radar or what? I throw an annoyed look in Liam's direction.

"I forgot my bag," he says quickly. He snatches up his bag and then darts down the stairs.

When Liam is out of eyesight, Logan licks his lips, and I can tell he is trying to hide a smile. "Guy doesn't seem very bright. You sure he can handle the job?"

"Yes."

"And you didn't think that maybe telling your boyfriend you're working with a guy was important?"

"No, I didn't. Because Liam is my assistant and nothing more. I haven't spent that much time thinking about him to know it was going to be an issue."

Logan's face lights up. "Well, that's good to hear."

His hand reaches around me and pulls me close. He locks his arms at my lower back and lifts me off the ground as he slips his tongue between my lips. The pleased sound that comes from his throat vibrates against my lips, tugging at my heart.

A horn honking outside breaks our kiss, and I swear he blushes. "We should get going." He gently places one more kiss to my lips before taking my hand and leading me down the stairs.

A warm breeze brushes my skin as we step outside. The sun is just starting to lower, leaving us with a beautiful cast of red and orange. Sunsets in Wyoming are one of the reasons I never left this state permanently. I can't imagine a better evening for tonight.

"I was thinking we should keep things more intimate tonight. Call me selfish, but I don't feel like sharing you with anyone, especially if this is the only night I'm going to get you to myself." He opens the passenger door of his truck for me and I freeze.

"I thought you were coming out tomorrow night after Kelsey's birthday dinner?"

"I was, but then your dad said he needed me at the bar tomorrow. I didn't know exactly why until you just told me I'm training Liam."

"I'll make sure we come in to see you after dinner."

A grin stretches across his face. "Sounds great."

I pull myself up into the truck and he closes my door. I relax back into my seat. Everything between us is so … normal. I wasn't sure what being apart would do to us, but clearly it does nothing. I'll be able to juggle this career/relationship better than I predicted.

Logan

"I thought you said we going to be alone tonight?" Sara asks.

I survey the park in front of us. A few months ago, the city started showing old movies every other Friday night in one of Wind Valley's parks. Tonight's film is *The Breakfast Club* and the park is full of people. Groups big and small fill the grass in front of the temporary screen. Some people are lying on blankets, some are in camping chairs, and a few have even gone as far to bring beanbags and small reclining chairs for their children

"We will be alone. I came earlier today while they were setting up the screen to scope out the place. I found the perfect spot in the trees over there." I point to our left. "It gives us a clear view of the screen and privacy."

Sara's smile beams and she rushes out of the truck. In good ole' fashion, she swings open the back door and starts unloading blankets and pillows. I rush around to help her before she tries to carry the entire load without my help.

"Oh wait! Let's take a picture real quick. I want one of our nights together, but I don't want to take my phone with me. No interruptions tonight." She half climbs back into the truck through the passenger door and I smile to myself as her legs dangle out the door. Damn, she sure does have a nice ass and that dress is riding up just far enough to be tempting, but still keep everything hidden. Her legs flutter as she leans more into the truck and her flip-flop falls off. She falls back to the ground and bounces in a circle on the foot that still has a shoe.

She giggles as she leans forward to pick it up. "If you'd been watching me with those eyes when you picked me up we'd never have made it here."

"That wouldn't have been a terrible idea." I step up behind her, wrapping my arms around her waist. I lean my head to the right and smile as she holds up the camera. Right before she touches the button, I turn to kiss her. I only reach her temple, but the way she stares at the finished photo tells me my choice was the right one. Sara looks up at me with watery eyes and I kiss her again. I'm going to kiss her as much as I can in the next two days. I have weeks to catch up on.

After she places her phone back inside the truck, I do the

same with my own. Then Sara grabs all the blankets in one big pile. I shake my head at her.

"What? I got this," she says and heads for the spot I picked in the trees.

I know she can do it on her own—they are just blankets after all—but she has me now. Her days of doing anything alone are gone. I jog up behind her and swing both her and the blankets into my arms. Attempting to be as romantic as I can, I carry her the rest of the way. I set out the blankets and pillow and Sara sits between my legs, leaning against my chest, as we settle in to watch the movie.

Everything about this moment is perfect. The girl in my arms is both my best friend and my girlfriend. I can talk to her about almost anything, but my worries about contacting my sister and Sara being in a whole other state with another guy —those issues will have to wait another night.

"Did you bring snacks?" she asks.

"Maybe, maybe not," I say and listen as she laughs. I squeeze her tighter and kiss the back of her head.

"I miss this stuff. The easy 'we can just be here and do nothing together' stuff."

"Me too. Tell your dad you quit and come home." I say it jokingly, but on the inside I'm serious.

"I wish I could do that, but I want this too much. I want to be successful now while I'm young."

"Yeah, but you're really young. Twenty-three is a little early to be planning retirement, isn't it?"

"No, not if one day I plan to start a family, and I want to make sure my career is set before kids happen."

I nod my head in silent agreement. Those exact words are what I should be saying to her. I should be the one working my ass off to make sure she has all those things. Maybe if I had been more driven in high school and not so focused on college life and parties, I'd be able to provide for her right now and we wouldn't have to be apart.

"I don't tell a lot of people this, especially not around my dad since he has that whole 'relationships ruin people' thing going on, and I guess I used to think he was right, but I want kids and a house and to be able to make enough money that I don't have to be on a schedule all the time. What about you— do you want kids someday?" she asks.

"If it's with you, I want everything."

Sara twists around, she studies me as a slight grin appears and then touches her lips to mine. She moves swiftly to straddle my lap and turns her soft kisses into passionate and desperate ones. I grab her hips to hold her in place as I slide my tongue past her lips. The movie starts in the background, louder than I'd anticipated but extremely appreciated at this moment because I have no intentions of stopping whatever Sara is about to initiate.

"I like this snack," she says, breaking the kiss and traveling kissing across my jawline. I love that she wants to be in control right now, but I can't let her do that. In this moment, I want to show her how much fun it is to lose control.

Lifting my hips, I push her up and then flip her over, wrapping my arm around her waist to lower her gently to the ground. A smile appears on her lips but I hide it when my mouth meets hers. One thing I've never understood, but will never complain about is how Sara has always carefully planned her life out. She's polite and caring and considerate of others. All those things together, I would never think that sex in a public place would be an option for her. Yet, it happens with us all the time.

I pepper kisses from her lips to her ear, tugging on the lobe and sucking. A hum of pleasure is barely audible from her lips, but her grinding hips are louder than any noise. Inching my fingers up her thigh, I grab hold of one leg, pulling it to the side, and let myself fall between her legs. Her back arches the moment my hand moves from her outer thigh to her inner one. I slide my hand toward her core, but before I reach it, she pulls me up, latching her lips onto mine. She tries to flips us over, but I hold my position. If she thinks I'm going too slow, I'll change that.

I pin her between me and the ground with just enough pressure to keep her from trying that again. Then I skip the slow movement and place my hand right where she needs it. Pulling her panties to the side, I slide two fingers into her. She moans loudly, but I know no one can hear it but me. Her hands spring from my hair to my jeans as she makes quick work of the buttons. Pulling them down just far enough to make people still think my pants are on, I remove my fingers and enter her slowly.

Fully inside her warmth, I kiss her hard and thrust into her harder. It's easy to lose myself when I'm with Sara.

CHAPTER TEN

Logan

It took everything I had to get out of Sara's bed this morning. It took even more work for me to leave her this afternoon and come to work. I don't want to be here because I dread spending any time with Liam. I'm usually pretty cool with everyone, but there's something about this guy. He just shows up out of nowhere and all the sudden lands a job working with Sara every day. Then, after one week, he's traveling home with her. Even if he isn't staying with her, something about this entire situation doesn't seem right. Either something is going on, or I'm jealous and can't handle the fact they work together alone. They may be just coworkers, but I don't like it. And I really don't like that I'm the one training him.

A passing car and chatter outside brings my attention to the door opening.

Look at him. Walking in here like he owns this place. Thinking he's all fancy with his clothes cleaned and pressed. I hold back my laugh. Doesn't he know he works in bar now?

Something is going to get spilled on him before the night is over. I roll my eyes as I catch him smiling at a few girls like a professional player. Disgusting. Real men don't act like that. They are calm and cool, like me—in every other moment of my life but this one.

I watch him with intensity as he steps closer to me. I'm standing behind the bar. I don't like this guy, and there was no way for me to hide it. I won't try to be friends with him or even get to know him. All I have to do is train him—that doesn't require me to be nice to him.

Shit.

I hold back another eye roll as Sara's dad follows Liam into the bar. My fists tighten as I realize I'm going to have to play nice until her father leaves. He scans the room on his way to the bar. His eyes stop on me.

Force a smile, Logan.

Do it!

"Liam, Dean." I reach out to shake both their hands. "Good to see you again."

"Oh, you've already met?" Dean sounds surprised. He tilts his head, but his eyes remain on me. I nod and he looks to Liam.

"Yeah, yesterday at Sara's apartment," Liam shares with him in a cheery tone. "Logan was picking her up for a date, and I just happened to be leaving at the same time."

"I'm surprised you made it to my house in one piece."

He's staying with her family?

"Of course." Liam gives a slight chuckle but glances my way with questioning eyes. "Any friend of Sara's is a friend of mine."

Friends, Logan. Liam even said it himself: they are just *friends*.

Dean watches me for a moment. He can give some pretty intimidating looks and I'm positive he can read my mind. He knows I don't like Sara and Liam working together. The fact I just learned he's staying with her family isn't helping. Obviously this new guy already has her father's approval, and me, I'm still busting my ass to earn it. I really want to look away from his gaze, but I don't. I can't let him or anyone see any signs of weakness.

"Alright," Dean says, clapping his hands and then rubbing them together. "Since we don't need to cover introductions and I assume my daughter filled you in on Liam's role with her new bar, I trust you will teach him everything you can in the one night."

"Yes, sir."

Teach him on the busiest night of the week? Yeah, Dean, no problem.

"And, since you can't train him on his whole job in one night, I plan to bring him back throughout the summer until we are confident he can run the place without supervision."

Yes! That means Sara will be coming home more too.

"In the meantime, Sara will be training him in Colorado, along with other new employees. Things are growing busier by the minute with the Silver Tap." Dean smiles wide. "That girl is going to be successful. I will do anything I can to help her."

Yeah, anything that means keeping her away from me. I'm not the idiot he thinks I am, but damn, I'm crazy about his daughter. I'll put up with this shit to have her in my life.

"Sara is one of kindest people I know—anyone would do

what they could to help her," I reply. He needs to know I'm as fully supportive of her career as he is.

"Then you better get started," he says, giving Liam a pat on the back before leaving us.

I step around the bar to Liam's side. We stand in the middle of the room as the door closes. The music has stopped playing and he glances as me with a half-smile, shrugs, and then looks away. Only dead silence and a shitload of tension follow. I glance at him one more time, keeping my eyes narrowed. He's not facing me anymore. Instead he's taking in the bar. His head starts to bob up and down.

"Did Sara give this place its look? If so, the place in Colorado is going to be a huge hit. I wonder if we can get a jukebox too," Liam says. "What do you think?"

I hate to admit it, but the tone of his voice almost convinces me he might actually only be here for a job. Nothing more.

"Sara is beauty and brains. The bar will be huge success either way," he adds.

Like I said, I was *almost* convinced.

Someone needs to set this guy straight. Warn him about his actions before it's too late. Seeing as how I would be the one to enforce punishment, it only seems right I explain the rules, too.

"Her father mentioned you recently started playing live bands again. What are your thoughts on doing that in Colorado? I mean, not right away, of course. If we added that to the list, Sara would be gone a lot longer, and we both know that is definitely not something she wants."

I nod my head. "Yeah, I think eventually it would be a great idea, but you definitely want to make sure you can bring in enough to compensate what you need to pay the bands. New businesses are hard to make those kinds of bets on. I have no doubt Sara will open a bar that's going to be a huge hit, but you still don't want to make those kinds of commitments until you have the facts."

"I completely agree. So, what are you going to train me on first?"

Yeah, okay, this guy might be harder to read than a girl. Either that, or he's one of those guys. The kind who is a ladies' man but oddly enough knows they aren't the man for your woman so they are just nice enough to make friends with her and you.

Fuck. This would be a whole lot easier if he were just an upfront dick. Now, I'm not sure what to make of him.

I open my mouth, but the sound of the door opening and a hysterical blonde running inside takes my full attention.

"Logan! Logan, I need the night off!" Abby says between sobs.

Looks like his first part of training is going to be how to deal with an overdramatic employee who finds the craziest ways to get out of work. I definitely don't have this part of the job perfected.

Abby just stares at me with black smudges running down her face. This could be one of two things. Either she was dumped or something bad really did happen. I'm going to go with option A, because it happens at least every other month.

I take two steps to meet her and she falls into me, burying her face in my chest. With my hands out at my sides I find myself in unfamiliar territory. My arms stay there, hanging in the air as I look back at Liam. For what, I don't know. Advice maybe. When he just stands there—something I notice he does a lot—a look of confusion hits his face. I let one hand gently pat her back.

"Um, it's okay, what happened?"

"I got dumped again!" she cries, pulling herself away and running toward the back room. I watch in silence until the back door slams closed, and I take a deep breath.

"Lesson one, don't hire females—got it." Liam chuckles. "How about we start my training after you handle that." He points behind me and I let out a sigh of defeat.

"I guess you can wait out here."

"Logan, seriously, that girl has got to pull it together. I can't work with her when she's like this." Beth comes out from the same room Abby just ran to. "You have got to tell her this is the last time she can pull this stint. Maybe tell her to stop dating all together."

I take another deep breath and look at my watch. It's only five. The bar won't be busy for a couple more hours. There are only a few people here now, all females focused on us, reminding me once again I need more guys working here. Still, I better take care of this before business picks up. Why can't Abby go about her job like everyone else? Half the time, I don't even notice who else is working because they aren't bringing attention to themselves.

"Hey"—I glance back at Liam— "how about you follow Beth for a bit?"

"I'd love to help." Beth smiles at Liam.

"Cool." Liam smiles back at her.

Interesting … maybe I could set these two up. That would sure take care of one problem.

Whoa.

Am I so afraid to lose Sara that I want to play match-maker? *Fuck.* What is wrong with me?

I shake the thought from my head. Right now I have bigger things to worry about. Abby sure as shit better have it together before Sara and the others get here. I have to show Sara I'm doing a successful job here while she's away, and having a crying employee isn't going to impress anyone.

Sara

I walk in to the BA and immediately my eyes and my heart search for Logan. When I don't spot him right away, my heart drops. I'm not getting to see him as much as I had planned this weekend. Go figure he has to train Liam the night of Kelsey's birthday party. Thank goodness Kelsey chose here of all places to spend it—I may have done some convincing to help with the decision. Otherwise, I'd only get to see Logan tomorrow before I leave and that is not okay with me.

"Where's Logan?" I ask Beth, who's behind the counter. I pretend to be distracted as I pull up a seat. I don't want Beth to think I'm desperate. Kelsey pulls up a seat next to me and Ethan follows on the other side of her. Some birthday party. It's been just the three of us since we left dinner. I should really not employ all my friends at the same place—this leaves no room for us to have nights off together.

"He's in the back. Abby came in a blubbering mess *again,* and he is trying to calm her down. I think this is the third time she has needed to have a 'moment' to pull herself together tonight. We thought she was good there for a couple hours, but something set her off again."

Beth's air quotes and annoyed tone don't go unnoticed. It's probably another ploy of Abby's to get Logan alone. I swear, that girl has had a crush since the day she set eyes on him. I don't blame her, I was the same way. The only difference is I didn't sleep with every man in the meantime.

"Don't do that." Beth shakes a finger in my face. "Don't make that sad face, and you suck in that bottom lip before he comes out here. This place is starting to pick up, and I don't need him getting all distracted. You being here is bad enough for the guy." She winks at me with a tight smile and then greets a few new customers who are sitting at the bar.

I watch her for a moment and then glance over to Kelsey. Am I really pouting? *Oh geez,* kissing already, I can't take these two anywhere.

"Whoa, you two, this is a bar, not a hotel." My eyes dart to the storage room. *How long does it take to calm her down?*

"Sorry, sometimes I just can't help myself when it comes to my wife. She's so damn beautiful."

I want to roll my eyes at them, but they deserve to be happy. After that stunt Ethan pulled this last year while I was away, he better tell Kelsey how beautiful she is every day, maybe even twice a day. He was such a scumbag. He's lucky we love him, or I would have never forgiven him.

"Aw, babe, you're pretty handsome yourself."

Okay. I can only handle so much of this when it involves my cousin.

"Stop it," I interrupt with a laugh. "At this rate, Clara won't be an only child for long. Hey, isn't your brother coming out tonight or was he just going to dinner because I'm thinking he is the perfect candidate to relieve Logan of whatever he has going on back there with Abby?"

"Sara, your family own this bar. You don't need anyone's permission to go back there."

Very good point.

I point to Kelsey and wink. I always knew there was a reason I liked her. Sliding off my stool, I casually make my way to the storage room. If I weren't in a bar full of people, I would totally be running to Logan. I'd tackle him in the storage room and do things to him that should never be done in public place. I laugh to myself and push open the door. Public places are starting to be our thing.

My humor is immediately gone when I see Abby wrapped in Logan's arms. My entire body heats and I swallow slowly before I jump to conclusions. Abby looks up at me over Logan's shoulder and a glint of happiness flashes in her eyes. *Oh, she would.* She totally planned this. I clear my throat. Logan turns around quickly and his eyes go big.

"Sara this isn't—"

I hold up my hand. "I know. Abby get back to work."

"But you're not—"

"Now, or this time I swear I will fire you, and I won't feel any guilt about it."

She stands there, next to Logan, and glances between us. A smile tugs at her lips before she steps away. "Thanks, Logan. You know how much I *love* your hugs."

Logan rolls his eyes and lets out a groan once she's left. "I swear, I am going to lose it on her soon. My patience with the woman has grown very thin the last few days. How many times can a girl call in for cramps or a breakup?"

I press my lips together to keep from laughing at him. Poor guy, that girl has been playing him. "Technically, I'd say none. You're just soft." I approach him slowly. Walking my fingers up his chest, I stop and wrap my arms around him. The tension in his body leaves at my touch.

Eww, now he smells like her.

Before I can think too much on this, I start bouncing and rubbing myself against him.

"Whoa, Sara, what're you doing?" Logan laughs. "Not that I mind it, but I do have a shift to finish, you know."

"You smell like her and I don't like it. You should smell like me."

His chuckle vibrates against me and I stop moving. He pulls me into a tighter hug and kisses my forehead. "I miss you."

"I miss you, too." I gaze up at him just in time for him to lean down and press his lips against mine.

"Er, should I come back?"

Regrettably, I pull my lips away. Liam is standing the doorway. I'd forgotten all about him. Weird, he always pops up at the *worst* moments.

"No, man, what's up?" Logan says, turning to face him but keeping me right at his side.

"There is a guy here, Conner I think, asking for you."

"Oh cool, tell him—"

"No, he asked for her," Liam says, pointing to me.

That's even weirder.

"I'll be right out," I tell him and he leaves us. Logan kisses my forehead once more and our moment alone is over. Reality is back in full swing.

Logan

Sara hasn't moved from her chair all night. When we

came out of the storage room, everyone had moved to a corner table by the window. Everyone being Connor, Ethan, Kelsey, and Sara. Things start to pick up fast. The band tonight is surprisingly good and pulling in more customers. Training Liam is pretty much pointless while it's busy, so I cut him after a few hours. That and Sara knows if I'm not teaching someone, I'll be off sooner. Unfortunately for me, Liam is now sitting at Sara's table enjoying her company while I work.

I'm working my ass off to avoid thinking of Sara and Liam. Exactly. There isn't even a Sara and Liam, but every time I hear her laugh reach across the bar, he is there, in her vision. Even if he isn't talking to her, just knowing he is getting to spend the evening in her company while I bust my back to make sure they have everything they need just rubs me the wrong way.

"You're doing it again," Beth coos behind me. I find her leaned against the wall as she dries the glass in her hand.

"Doing what?"

"Watching her. Radiating love from your eyes. Then, a fire burst into flames from your ears when you realized who is sitting next to her. Everyone is running for their lives, and all you care about is making sure he doesn't make out it alive."

No joke. I stare at her with my mouth open as I raise both eyebrows. She laughs. "Or you could just be annoyed because you wish you were sitting next to her."

"Yeah, wow, did you really just say all that? Where do you come up with this crap?" A laugh escapes my lips. Her visions, or whatever you want to call it, might not have been so far off. Maybe void the fire and my making sure someone dies, and it's a true story.

"I read a lot."

"Clearly sci-fi."

"No, romance novels can get intense, too, you know. It's not always sex and a bunch of guys."

I raise my left brow as I look at her.

"Okay, so it's mostly about sex and a bunch of hot guys. Hey, I hate to break it to you, but you are the manager here right now, and if you want to be off work, you could probably talk yourself into it. After all, it's pretty slow and I'll probably get more work done if you get out of my way. I can handle Abby. We were scheduled to close the bar together anyway. Thanks for that, by the way."

"You're right," I say, ignoring her last comment. I set down my towel, head to the back, and change my shirt. Then I walk right up to Sara's table to stand between her and Liam.

"It's about time you got off," Ethan cheers, holding his beer up. I give him a fist bump and then offer my hand to Sara.

"Feel like dancing?" I ask. She rises quickly, clearly approving of my idea as she pulls me onto the dance floor. Kelsey and Ethan follow, along with a few other customers. The band must notice the amount of couples on the floor because they quickly change the music to a slow song, playing their version of "More Than Words."

Sara's slender arms wrap around my neck as we sway back and forth. I enjoy the feel of her touch for a moment before I switch us to a more formal stance, showing her a few dance moves. She laughs softly as I twirl her, pulling her back against my chest.

Behind us, Ethan attempts the same move, but his arm

catches on Kelsey's forehead, causing them to stop dancing to laugh it off.

"I should never have left last summer," Sara admits, resting her cheek against me. I swallow, resisting the urge to ask her why she did. It's something I've asked myself over and over.

"Being with you scares me. I'm scared of the way I feel, how I think, the ideas I get. I think more of you than I do of my own future, and that terrifies me. I knew it then and I ran. I don't want to run this time. I want to make this work. Promise me you won't break my heart."

The music is still playing, but we've stopping moving. She leans back far enough to look up.

"I promise," I say, praying that I can keep it.

Leaning down, I kiss her as deeply as I can in front of everyone. I don't stop until the hoots and hollers around us cause Sara to giggle and dash for the door, tugging me behind her.

Sara slips her hand into mine and I squeeze it, pulling her close to my side. Late June in Wyoming is a great time of year. It's warm, but not too warm, a perfect sixty-five degrees and the wind is almost fully nonexistent. We walk in silence until we reach Sara's apartment building.

Living in the building next to hers was always fun, but right now I wish we didn't have to choose. Without saying a word, I wrap my arms around her shoulders and we head inside hers. For me, it doesn't matter whose place we pick, as long as I'm with Sara, I'm home.

CHAPTER ELEVEN

Sara

I hate Mondays. Not only because they mean the weekend is over, but because it's the day that signifies the beginning to a long week. The only plus side to a Monday right now is that each one is a day closer to my moving home. I should be thankful another week has come and gone, but right now, I'd rather rewind a day. Put myself back in Wind Valley. Not here, at the Silver Tap and moody as hell.

I know it's because I didn't wake up to Logan's face. I didn't wake up to his touch or to his smell. To arms wrapped around me. Everything is better with him. And everyone knows that when you're in a bummed out mood, time passes way too slowly and nothing productive gets done.

"Okay, so your first interview is at eleven—that's in twenty minutes. The next one's at one and then again at three today. Same for tomorrow and Wednesday." Liam pulls up a seat next to me at the bar. "How many people do you plan to hire right now?"

he asks, marking something down on the clipboard in front of him before flashing me a grin. "Oh, and the bank called. You need to sign some more papers that your father wired over first thing this morning, and I know you signed the liquor contract, but they haven't sent us a copy of the liquor license and we need that."

It's a good thing Liam is here to keep me on task.

Before I left Wind Valley, I made a few rules for myself. It's not that I don't trust myself or anyone else, but I made them to help Logan stress less. Even though he has no idea what these rules are or that I even have them.

One of the rules is to never be in a closed space alone with Liam. The office is too small of a space. All our work will forever be done at the bar top, and I sit in the seat one over from his.

"I was thinking six for now," I say. "We can get three in to start training right away, and the other three can come in about a month before opening. I'll want twelve to fifteen total, but the others can wait till we at least have glasses and stuff to train with. And I'll take care of that other stuff at some point today."

"Did you make those plans or did your father?"

I smirk at him. "What plans? And do you really need to ask? You and I both know if I had my way, I'd hire as many people as it took to get this place ready and open in the next week."

"Yeah, I'm surprised your dad is moving things as slowly as he is anyway. That and I thought he gave you this bar, but it doesn't really sound like it."

Something in Liam's words hits a sore spot. This *is* my bar, or at least it will be. As soon as those papers come in.

"Are the three interviews today your friends?" I ask, changing the subject.

Liam has a few buddies who want part-time jobs and I agreed to interview them. Two of them are in a band. Liam's idea is to hire them now as bartenders and later promote them as our official Saturday night band if things turn out well. His plan is one I like and one that might possibly check two things off the opening list. I just hope his friends are as responsible as Liam. I want a fun and laid-back place to hang out, but I also need people who can keep the place running.

"Well, two today and one tomorrow. I hope you know you don't have to hire them for my sake. Everything is 100 percent your call."

"Oh I know." We both laugh at my lack of hesitation to respond. "I'm sure they will be just fine."

"Knock, knock."

The front door opens and a tall man walks in. His shaggy hair is clearly dyed black from a box, his left eyebrow has three piercings, and his nose has one of those bullrings through it. At first glance he is a little intimidating, but he smiles and aims a mouth full of bright, white teeth our way, relaxing me a bit. He has on an outfit entirely in black and loud boots that clunk as he drags his feet. He strides toward us without waiting for our greeting, and when he reaches us, he extends his hand toward Liam.

"You must be the boss around here. I'm Mark; I have an interview with you." He glances at me and winks. His jaw moves quickly as he chomps on what I hope is gum. "Damn, if you are any sign of the fine-ass women I could be working with, I better make sure I nail this interview."

My jaw drops and my eyes go wide. Is this guy for real? I cannot seriously interview him now.

"Well, you just lost any opportunity at an offer." I say with a clipped tone.

Liam steps forward and begins to show the man out.

"You're shittin' me! You're going to let her speak to me that way?" Mark looks to Liam.

"I'm not the boss. She is," Liam says in a firm voice and then slams the door closed behind him. He raises his hands in the air. "Not my friend. I swear."

"I sure hope not." I laugh. "Did that really just happen?"

"Yeah, it did. And what a dick for assuming I'm the boss."

"It doesn't surprise me."

Liam nods. "Oh, now you're judging the guy who was judging you?" He chuckles. "What's next on our agenda?"

I stand and clap my hands together. "We shop for décor and hope that my next two interviews are much better than that one. Oh, and will you please be here for the interviews over the next few days? I don't want to …" My voice trails off because I don't want to go into detail on what could have happened without Liam.

"Of course," he says and his eyes meet mine. "I won't let anything happen to you."

* * *

"Hi, you must be Sara." A woman about five foot five, same as me, greets me. "I'm Andi, Liam's friend," she says, tucking her A-line, black hair behind her ear.

"I am." I smile and reach forward to shake her hand. "Please, have a seat." I point to the bar top where I was sitting when she came in. My chair screeches when I pull it out and hers does the same, sending a shiver down my spine. It's like nails on a chalkboard. *We really need to get pads under these stools.*

"So, Liam tells me you're the lead singer in a band. That must take a lot of responsibility," I start right away.

"I am, and yes, it does. I started out as a guitar player. Then the lead vocal got pregnant with the other guitar player's baby. Now she's a stay-at-home mom and I've been singing for two years."

"Oh, wow. This is an odd question, and for the record, it isn't part of your interview, but is it normal to have relationships with other band members? I mean, it's kind of like they are your coworkers, right? Has that ever caused any problems?"

Alright, so this is sort of a work-related question. I'm not big on coworkers forming relationships. It's not good for business. Bad breakups usually include new hires after someone quits. Kelsey and Ethan were the exception. And Logan and I, too.

Damn. I really have to enforce this rule. I don't want to go into this thinking I'll have a band here only to find out they broke up from something silly.

"Well, Jim replaced me as a guitarist and he's already married. Brian and Kathy, she was the last vocalist, are married now, Lewis plays the drums and he's single. He is usually the one who brings in the ladies. So we don't have to worry about anyone hooking up and breaking us up. If I weren't into women, I would totally be into Lewis, but as of right now he isn't my type." She shrugs like it's no big thing. Which, it isn't.

"Oh, well, that's great to hear," I say, glancing at the paper in front of me. I should get on with the interview before I start to come off as creepy. Although I may have already passed that point. "Before we begin, do you have any questions?"

"Nope. Let's do this thing. This would really be a neat place to work. And Liam was right about you."

I hesitate before asking, "What did he say about me?"

"That you were kind, honest, and would make me comfortable."

I smile.

"He also said you were beautiful and smarter than people actually give you credit for. He's a nice guy. You did well in hiring him." I sit there for a moment just watching her. Liam really said all those things?

I force myself to get back on track before I spend her entire interview chatting about our friends and before I know it, her interview is over and she leaves.

"Hey, how did it go? I kept the office door cracked to listen, but honestly I wasn't too concerned with anything going wrong. Andi can kick any male or female ass."

I turn to Liam. "I believe it."

"So, ready for your next one?"

"As long as they turn out just like her, I sure am."

"Grayson is one of my closest friends, and he will bring in a lot of female cliental, I promise. But even so, he's a great guy. You'd be smart to hire him." Liam snaps his fingers and claps his hands. "Well, I better go get that liquor order you made out."

I'm starting to think there is entire side to Liam I don't know about. I'm not even sure I should know about it, considering I'm his boss and I'm dating Logan, but if I'm honest with myself, Liam is becoming a friend. I trust him and I feel comfortable around him. He really is a nice guy who I'm thankful to have working for me, and I don't want to do anything to ruin that.

Logan

This has been the longest week of my life. I work hard to guarantee I'm home when Sara calls me. Except every one of her calls have been past midnight. She says it's because they have been working late. She told me she hired a few more people to start working part time next week to help her and Liam put the place together. I feel like a dick for suggesting they hire someone to come in and take care of things like wall décor, tables, stocking the storage room, or even organizing her office so that she doesn't need to be in Rockland, but Sara said that isn't what they did with the BA and it isn't what they are going to do now. I see her point and I understand that doing it herself assures it gets done by the day she wants it done, but work can also be an excuse for hiding the truth. *What if she isn't really working because she is with Liam?* What am I saying—she's with him either way. *Is that the reason she can't come home for 4th of July weekend?*

"Logan?"

My head snaps up. Conner is standing my kitchen, a duffle bag hanging over his shoulder and another held up by his left hand.

"Ethan told you I was moving in today, right?" he asks. "I knocked, but you didn't answer."

"Yeah I was—" I point to the TV. It's off.—"sorry, man, I must have really been zoning out."

"It's cool," he says, glancing around. "Left or right?"

"Left."

Conner makes his way down the hall without looking back. I rub my neck and push off the couch. I need a distraction. Between not talking to Sara and Tyler not texting me back with an update on my sister, I'm going crazy.

"Do you have more stuff to move in?" I say loudly enough for Conner to hear me.

"Just another bag of clothes."

Well, that idea's out.

"You want to go see if there is a game we can join in at the rec?" I ask. Shooting some hoops sounds like a great de-stressor.

"Yeah, give me just a minute."

Connor steps out of his new room in shorts and a cut-off shirt, ready to go.

"How's Sara doing in Colorado?"

"Good."

"Just good?"

"Yep." What more can I say when I barely speak to her? "The opening is still on schedule" is what I come up with.

"We should go down there one of these weekends. Check out the competition in the area."

I nod. That isn't a half-bad idea.

CHAPTER TWELVE

Sara

"My father's on his way here."

"Right now?" Liam asks. "This place isn't ready yet—it's getting close, but not yet. I thought he said he wasn't coming back until the place was finished."

"Yep, I know. I told him that much, but he insisted."

My father hasn't been here once since he moved me here. I have no idea why he thinks he needs to come now. He knows the bar isn't ready. I really hope this isn't his way of trying to prove I can't do this. It wouldn't be like him to act that way with me. He's taught me everything I know about this business. If anything, he's coming to see if I was paying attention all these years.

"He didn't say anything to you over the weekend we were there, did he?" I ask, since Liam was staying with my father— which I still think is weird.

"Nope. He mentioned something once about distractions and how if you keep letting them get in the way, it's going to set things back. But I wasn't actually part of that conversation and didn't catch it all, so I didn't ask about it. Probably shouldn't have even told you since I have no idea what he was talking about."

"He thinks I'm distracted? But everything is on schedule. Nothing has happened to delay the opening."

Liam shrugs. "Yeah, like I said, I probably missed the main part of that discussion."

"Well, who was he talking to?"

"I don't know. I just turned around and went back to the guest room."

What's my father thinking? Nothing is distracting me. I'm doing everything that he wants me to do. That could have been the reason he had Liam stay with me in Rockland this weekend, instead of going up to Wind Valley, so I wasn't distracted. Sometimes I really wish I knew what was going on in his mind, but at the same time, if I'm this paranoid when things go as planned, I can't even imagine what process his mind goes through.

"I'm sure if it was something important, he would tell you."

"Well I'd hope so," I say. "Let's get some things done in here to make it look presentable. I don't feel like giving him anything to say today."

* * *

I watch in almost pure agony as my father walks around the bar. He's going slowly and making sure to inspect everything he sees. It's driving me mad. Liam is standing next to me trying to hide a smile. He knows how stressed I get when my father is around. One mistake and my entire career path could be taken away from me. Yeah, I'd still have a business degree, but I I'd have to find a whole new business to be in. I'd have to start over from scratch with nothing, and I don't want that. I don't think I could handle working from the ground up. I don't care if I sound selfish. My father may have started this business, but for the last two years I've done a damn good job helping him keep it running. If it weren't for me and maybe Ethan handling the BA last year, Dad wouldn't even have this place to open right now. My place. *Damn it.* I better start acting like the boss.

"Dad, maybe we should go get lunch. You had a long drive, and I'm sure working isn't what you wanted to do the moment you got out of your car."

"Nonsense, someone needs to keep you on your toes. If I didn't come here to check on you, I doubt this place would look as clean as it does. There would probably be papers all over the bar top—your signature way of keeping things orga- nized that no one but you can figure out. There would prob- ably be boxes lying around the entire space instead of neatly organized in rows on the wall over there. I know you better than you think, Sara. Next time I come, maybe I should tell you I'm going to be working in the office so you'll finally purchase those filing cabinets I keep telling you to get."

"Actually, Dean, those cabinets have already been ordered."

"Really?" My father beams at Liam, as do I. *He ordered cabinets?*

Liam nods. "Yep. And those boxes have actually been organized for a week now. We took care of that when we came back from Wind Valley. You'd be impressed at the steps

Sara has taken since I started here. I've only suggested we do it sooner rather than later."

A smile creeps on my father's face as he stares at Liam. It's a little unsettling.

"I knew there was a reason we met. You're exactly the kind of man my daughter needs."

My face scrunches up at his comment. *Because he ordered cabinets?*

"She isn't one to ask for help, so she needs someone who is going to step up and make those decisions for her." My father gives Liam a pat on the shoulder. "You're going to fit into this family just fine."

"Family?" Liam and I both say, confused.

"Yeah, eh, you know, the bar business family."

Liam chuckles uncomfortably, but I just keep looking at my father.

He glances away and heads for the door. "Alright you two, let's go get some lunch," he says.

"Good. I'm starving," Liam says as the door closes behind my father. He nudges my shoulder. "Don't look so surprised and ignore his comment. It kind of makes me feel like a loser."

"Why?" I ask, trying to figure out what's going on because the things he's pointed out actually do make it look like I've been distracted.

"Because I didn't come up with those ideas, ordering the cabinets or telling you we need to organize the boxes so when the storage room is ready we can unpack them easier. Logan told me I should do those because he had a feeling you would overlook them. He said you're great with the big picture, but you space out a lot on the little things. He's also the one who came up with the suggestion to hire my band friends now because they could be useful later. He's a smart guy."

The small mention of his name and the thought that Logan is training Liam how to help me accomplish everything I need to before this place opens warms my heart. My dad isn't giving Logan enough credit. I sure wasn't. I blink back the tears that sting my eyes. *Great, I miss him even more now.*

Logan

The words on my laptop computer screen are starting to blur together. I pinch the spot between my eyes and take breath. Tyler was again able to hack into the system of the children's home we went through and get me the address in Nevada where my sister is still living with her foster parents. It's the same damn address I've been sending letters to and the same damn address they keep coming back from, unopened. If they're anything like the family I was set with, she isn't getting her way at all. She's nineteen now; she should be moved out and on her own. Something doesn't add up.

Groaning, I shut the computer down and stretch, popping my neck in the process. I need a break from this. Maybe I need to rethink the entire situation. What if she doesn't want to see me? What if I'm trying too hard for something that isn't there? She was little when we were split up—does she even remember having a brother?

"Hey, man," Conner says, stepping into the kitchen. "You've been sitting at that table for hours. Don't you think you should get up at some point?"

He opens the fridge, twists the cap off the orange juice with his name on it, and drinks.

"Yeah, just trying to take care of some stuff," I say, standing.

"It looks like something important. Want to talk about it?"

"It's a long story."

Conner watches me for a moment before he nods his head. "Yeah, cool, another time maybe."

"Yeah," I say. Then we just stand there, looking at each other and making an already awkward conversation even weirder.

"Okay, so I'm going to head out. Shift starts in an hour. You coming in tonight?" Conner asks, turning for his room.

"I think so. It's either that or sit around here doing nothing."

"Cool, see you there."

* * *

Four hours later, I pull up a seat at the bar top. Conner nods his greeting, twisting off the top to a bottle of dark beer and sliding it my way.

"Slow night," he says.

I nod, taking a sip.

"You can always depend on the regulars."

"We've got to depend on someone." He chuckles, stepping away to meet Beth, who joins us with a tray full of empty glasses.

Conner and Beth work easily together. I schedule them on the same shift a lot because they are a strong team. Abby works well, too, even if she keeps flirting with Conner like she's doing right now. Beth just rolls her eyes every time Abby speaks. Most days I couldn't care less, but days like today, days when I haven't spoken to Sara but five minutes, makes me wonder what goes on in the mind of a woman.

"This seat taken?" His voice booms in the almost empty bar.

"Dean," I greet him. "What brings you down here?"

"I just thought I would see how things are going. Check up on the place. Do you come here on all your nights off?" he asks, declining a beer and requesting a water from Conner.

Great. He's probably thinking I'm a drunk or something.

"Just on the nights I feel like it," I say. *Damn it, that sounded stupid.*

"Well, let's hope you don't feel like it too often."

With a closed-mouth smile, I nod and then take a long pull from my drink.

"No, sir."

An awkward silence falls between us as I drink my beer and he his water. I set the empty glass down and Conner signals for another. I shake my head "no" even when another beer is exactly what I need.

Every subject Sara's father likes flashes through my head as I try to think of something to talk about. I've never been in a situation with him where we didn't have anything to talk about. Maybe now would be a good time to ask for his approval to marry his daughter. Not exactly planned and very early, but I'm confident of her answer. After she opens the Silver Tap and moves back to Wind Valley, of course.

"So, Sara seems to enjoy Colorado," I start. I'd better ease into this conversation.

"Yeah, I think so too. I actually just got back to town from visiting her." He nods. "She's done a fabulous job. She's surrounded by good people. Smart people. People who could take her places."

I shake what I'm taking as insult from my head. *Don't let him get under your skin.*

"Sara brings out that side of people." I sip my water. "She did it with me; I have no doubt she could do it with anyone else."

I feel his eyes on me, but I don't turn to face him. *Keep it cool, Logan.* He's probably trying to decide if he believes me, if he thinks I've changed, or how he's going to change the subject again to bring me down.

"I suppose that's true" is what he says instead.

I pinch my lips together to hold back my smile. *I stumped him.*

My immature side wants to laugh at this stupid conversation. I mean, come on. I can't hold a conversation with my girlfriend's father. How lame does that make me?

"Liam's turning out to be quite the gentleman, and he's doing a fine job being there for Sara. I'm happy we found him. She needs someone like him around to keep her on track."

And just like that, it's a punch to the gut as he insults me, again. I've always known Dean doesn't like me, but when he says things like this, I know without a doubt he's trying to push Sara and me apart. I want to tell him, "Too bad. You'll have to find another way to make Liam part of your family." But instead, I stand and lay some cash on the bar.

"She's sure one lucky woman," I say. "Have a great night, Mr. Connelly." I'll have to get his permission another time.

CHAPTER THIRTEEN

Sara

Sitting alone inside the Silver Tap, I'm able to absorb the bar's atmosphere and feel proud of how far it's come. The music box arrived last week. Liam set it up right away because working in silence has been miserable. I turn the set on random and pull up a seat at the bar. Without Liam here, I don't have to be on top of things. He's a dedicated worker and I'm proud he's on the team, but I miss taking a few minutes to just do nothing. *Nothing but play on my phone.*

I tap the screen to my Instagram account and the most up-to-date photo is of Clara blowing a spit bubble. I scroll through a few more and stop when I get to one of Logan. He's got his arm wrapped around Ethan, who is holding Clara. They're standing outside Kelsey and Ethan's house. From the sweat glowing off his face, they were more than likely shooting hoops.

I stare at the photo. I miss that smile. Those lips. The way his arms flex when he holds me. I even miss those times after he and Ethan have played ball for hours when he wraps his sweaty arms around me and doesn't let me go until I've kissed him. A smile touches my lips at the memory. That was another sneaking around moment. I can't wait to share those moments in front of people. It's only been two weeks since I saw him and I'm going crazy.

"Hey, girl," Andi's voice startles me.

"Hey," I breathe as I set my phone down and twist in my chair. She doesn't need to know I was ogling Logan's picture.

She pulls up a seat and I hand her the keys she came to pick up.

"Thanks," she says, watching me with a puzzled look on her face.

"What?" I ask. I've only been around Andi a handful of times, but she's always been easy for me to talk to. In a way, I think she is going to be my Colorado Kelsey.

"The look on your face is a little depressing," she says. "Do you have a special someone back home? You look totally bummed out right now, and guessing a guy has something to do with it is usually right 98 percent of the time."

"Is it really that obvious?"

"Yes, it is. You look mopey," she says. "When was the last time you saw him?"

"Two weeks ago." I shrug. "I was supposed to go home and see him this weekend, but Liam went instead."

She doesn't miss a beat. "Why didn't you go?"

"My father thought it would be best if Liam went to get more training."

"But don't you own this bar, don't you get to make the decisions on how he's trained?" she points out quickly. *Has she been planning these questions?* "You should get to make those decisions, right?"

I should, yes, but not until I get those papers. I smile, not wanting to get into that discussion with her.

"Hmm, you have a pretty good point there, rookie," I say. "You might just be my favorite employee right now."

"I'm basically your only employee right now." She laughs. "Besides the other people you hired and Liam, but I don't know how much he counts as an employee of yours since he is always doing what your dad says. How does that work anyway? Do you guys share this place or what? Why's he setting most of the rules, and why is he controlling Liam's training?"

I freeze and stare blankly at her. Now that she mentions it, my father does seem to be controlling most of what Liam does and something isn't right about the ownership papers taking this long. I press my eyelids closed and drop my chin to my chest. Please do not let this be another one of my father's schemes to keep Logan and me apart. I've been denying it since the day I got here, but enough is enough.

"My father's a smart man. He has a plan for everything," I tell her. "I seek his advice every now and then, and it makes sense to have Liam train in a fully functioning bar if he's going to be managing this place on his own."

"Okay." She hops off the stool and heads for the door. "I won't pry anymore because I need to get going, but it's Friday. Just go home. What are you going to get done here that you can't get done there?"

Nothing crosses my mind.

"I just might do that," I tell her, still staring at the door after she's left. *Why didn't I think of that?*

My ringing phone grabs my attention. I let the unfamiliar number go to voicemail because I'm that girl. I screen any call that comes from a number I don't recognize. Immediately my phone chirps with a voicemail. I punch in the password as I gather my purse. If I want to get on the road, I'd better start packing now.

Resting my phone between my ear and shoulder, I lock the door just as the voicemail begins to play.

"Hi, Ms. Connelly. This is Allen with Feature Your Cable Company. I am calling to confirm the setup for tomorrow morning. Arrival time should be anywhere between nine and eleven. If you have any questions, please don't hesitate to call me on my cell, (303) 859-1597. Have a great day."

The voicemail ends and I stand motionless on the sidewalk outside the bar. *So much for visiting Logan this weekend.* I start heading for my place again when it occurs to me, I may not be able to see Logan, but I sure can call that lawyer and find out what's taking so long to transfer ownership.

Logan

Inviting Liam to stay with me this weekend is a huge step for me. I want to like him for Sara's sake, but at the same time, I still see him as competition. I don't like competition. I'm confident Sara loves me and only me, but I'm no idiot to deny that unplanned things happen. And with Liam being the one who's there with her, I still don't trust him, and I definitely don't want to give him a reason to think he has the upper hand.

So finding Abby inside my apartment the second Liam

and I step inside is the last thing I want to deal with, and it sure as fuck doesn't look good.

"Abby, what're you doing here?" I say, groaning the moment I see her sitting my couch. My voice is firm, but I don't care. "And could you please put some pants on?"

"What do you mean, Logan?" She rolls her eyes at me.

"I mean, why are you are on my couch?" I ask, attempting to stay calm. "And go put on some pants."

I throw a blanket at her and then turn off the TV, tossing the remote onto the couch next to her. Dammit, Conner. I swear, if he's hooking up with her, I'm going to beat his ass. I warned him about her and yet, here she is, in *my* apartment.

This definitely doesn't look good.

"Stop acting like you don't know why I'm here." She grabs the remote and turns the TV back on. Then she rests her feet on my coffee table and crosses her ankles. "Hey, Liam." She winks and then removes the blanket covering her body. I close my eyes and take a deep breath. This is a crazy amount of trouble. I rub my hands down my face and shrug at Liam. I still don't understand why she's wearing only a t-shirt. Probably means Conner is around here somewhere. I glance around the apartment. He's nowhere to be found. Where the fuck is Conner? This is not what I wanted to come home to.

"Hey, Abby," Liam says back and the tone in his voice is a dead giveaway that he is uncomfortable. "Um, Logan, I can just give Sara's dad a call and go stay with them for the weekend. It's really not a big deal."

"No," I say firmly and then pin Abby with another heated glare. I can't have him calling Sara's dad and telling him the reason he couldn't stay with me was because there was another woman on the couch. That would not go over very well. I have to figure out what is going on, and I have to get her out of here pronto.

"Okay! I got groceries and I got movies, this is going to be one—oh, hey, man." Conner pauses when he's fully through the apartment door and gives me an unsure smile. He sets the bags down and rubs the back of his neck. "So hey"—he points to the hallway—"I need to talk to you about something."

"Yeah, I think you do," I say. "Liam, make yourself at home. This won't take long." Abby immediately offers him the remote.

"Here, you can pick out something for us to watch."

I don't look back to see if he accepted her offer or not because I'm too fumed and ready to punch someone by the time I make it outside with Conner.

"What the fuck is going on? Why is she here?" I demand once the door closes behind me.

"She needed a place to stay, and I know I just moved in, but I felt bad for her. Her boyfriend cheated on her." The look in his eyes shows real concern. *Poor guy.* She probably played him like a fool just to get into my apartment. For me or for him, I have no idea, but I'm not letting her stay to find out.

"You do realize this is the same girl who helps multiple guys cheat every week, right? She is also the same girl who slept with Tyler when he cheated on your sister!" My voice grows louder.

"That was a long time ago, Kelsey is over it and besides Abby seems happy right now."

"Yeah, because she is sitting on my couch! I know she is up to something and I swear it's something bad. She wants to split Sara and me up, and I'll be damned if I'm going to let this relationship go down in flames all because of her. There's no way Sara will say yes to marriage if I let Abby stay here for any amount of time." My arms are in the air and I'm pacing. When Conner doesn't say anything, I stop to look at him.

His eyes are wide and he's making a stuttering sound. "Did … what … did you really just say that you're going to propose? To Sara? Is this for real or are you just going that crazy right now?"

Fuck.

I said it out loud?

"I —" My eyes dart around like I'm going to find the rest of my sentence on a sign nearby. When I don't come up with anything, Conner claps his hands together once.

"Dude! Congrats! Why haven't you told anyone, and what the fuck is up with everyone keeping the idea of marriage a secret? Don't you people know that we're all family and friends and we support each other? I mean, fuck, my sister didn't even invite me to her wedding."

I can't help but chuckle. "Yeah, it would seem to be the trend these days. You started it when you went off and had a kid without telling anyone."

"Hey, that wasn't my fault. His mother neglected to tell me she even had a kid. I was just as much in the dark as the rest of you." A small smile appears on his face, but it quickly turns down.

"She still won't let you see him?" I ask.

"She will, but she doesn't think I live in a safe environment for a kid."

"Seriously? The police station is like two blocks away."

"I told her that, but she just won't have it. Not unless she's here with him anyway. I even asked if living with Kelsey would make a difference, but she refuses to answer me. I'm running out of ideas here." He looks defeated and lost. I wish I could help him. Or that I had advice for him. I just don't think I have a place to say anything, considering my father never fought this hard to get to know me. Hell, as far as I know, my father never even tried to find me. He might not even know about me.

Abby's laugh sounds through the apartment window.

"Having a girl like Abby around isn't going to help your situation," I say, much calmer this time. "Or mine for that fact."

"I know, and I'll make sure she knows this is temporary. She can sleep in my room while Liam is here, but can we please just give her a few days to sort some things out? She says she can cook. Like really cook." His eyes widen and he looks excited. A few home-cooked meals might be nice. And I guess she is still technically my friend and I can't just kick her out. I sigh. Conner really isn't leaving me with any other choice.

"She has one week." I hold up a finger and then turn for the door. "And you are going to make sure she knows it," I shout over my shoulder.

I had better call Sara before Liam does. *Fuck.* How do I get myself into situations like this? I have got to start telling everyone no. Everyone but Sara, that is.

CHAPTER FOURTEEN

Sara

"I have to tell you something and I'm not sure how to say it." Liam stands across me with his chin resting against his chest.

It's Friday again and he had suggested going back up to Wind Valley this weekend, too. I've opted to go in his spot and told him to take the weekend off, but by the way he's acting right now, I suspect that plan might have to change.

"What's wrong?"

"I, uh, let me think for a second on how I want to phrase this."

"Okay …" This is starting to sound like it might be something juicy. Maybe he's seeing someone, or maybe Andi met a new girl. Or maybe—

"When I was in Wyoming last weekend, there was a girl in Logan's apartment."

I freeze. Liam's eyes dart around the bar for a minute

before they come back to mine. *It was probably Kelsey there with Ethan.*

"And?" I ask before returning to placing the artwork where it will eventually need to go on the bar's walls. I'm not really sure how I'm supposed to react in a situation like this, but the fact I just starting sweating isn't a good sign.

"Well, it kind of sort of looked like she was moving in."

Again, I freeze and turn to look at him.

"What do you mean?"

I bet Conner has a new girlfriend.

"I mean move in, like bags packed and her lying in what I think were pajamas on the couch"

Huh.

"Did you get her name?" I ask. "He lives with Conner, so I bet it was someone he knows."

Liam doesn't answer right away, and I swear his face get more pale as I stare at him.

"Liam, what's wrong?"

"It was Abby."

I step back as if someone slapped me.

"Abby, like the Abby we work with?"

He nods.

I flip around to face the wall and mutter a quick "fuck" under my breath. I've always known she was a little off in the man department, but she can't seriously be dumb enough to first go after my cousin while he was with Kelsey and now try Logan. If she isn't careful, she isn't going to have many friends left.

After taking a few focus breaths, I turn around, again.

"Oh, that's no big deal," I say. The words sound fake even to me.

"Yeah, that was real convincing." He laughs. "But hey, if it helps, he didn't seem too thrilled about it, and from what I gathered he didn't even know about it."

My jaw drops.

"Start with that next time!" I yell and smile at the same time. Now that sounds like the Logan I know. I knew there wasn't anything to worry about.

"I wasn't trying to upset you, but it was last week. Don't you think it's a little weird that he hasn't mentioned it yet?"

"Abby isn't someone we like to talk about."

"Okay. One other thing I noticed while I was there."

"What's that?" Nothing could be worse than what he just said.

"Logan went out both nights I was there. He didn't drink, but he still went out."

"Okay," I say, confused on his sudden interest in Logan's behavior. And it's not a very good one either.

"You haven't been out once since you've been here. Or at least if you have, I haven't noticed."

"I'm not really a big party kind of person." My going-away party last year was the last time I drank, and I'm happy with that.

"You don't have to party to go out."

"No, I know, but most going out involves drinking."

"You don't like drinkers?" Now he's dazed.

"I don't like who a person becomes once they've been drinking."

"But you own a bar?"

"Just because I don't like it doesn't mean I don't want people to have fun. I'm one of a kind when it comes to my drinking theory. I also like owning a place where I can watch over my customers and make the calls. If I think they've had enough, I can cut them off and call them a cab. I'm a very dedicated bar owner. I take care of my customers."

"Do you have a deal with a cab company or something?"

"No."

"You should."

I stare at Liam as he goes back to unpacking more boxes with décor in them. He really does come up with some great ideas. The Silver Tap is going to be in good hands when I leave. *Leave.* The idea gets me choked up, but it's not a surprise. I've just grown to enjoy the people here the same way I enjoy the people in Wind Valley. Staying here for the weekend here won't hurt anyone.

Logan

"Abby, is this for real?" I shout into the hallway. I have got to stop sharing a bathroom with her. I was trying to be polite, but she and Conner are just going to have to suck it up.

"What? I can't dry that stuff in the dryer. It'll shred it up." She huffs, her hands on her hips in the doorway.

"There's nothing to shred!" I yell. "Get it out, get it out right, now."

"Jesus, Logan. You're such a dick. I have no idea what Sara sees in you," she says, yanking her panties off the shower rod and stomping out the bathroom.

"You're sharing 100 percent with Conner from now on!"

"Whatever!"

I open my mouth to argue more because I've been in a dick mood ever since Sara called to cancel her trip home and yelling is helping. Abby lucks out on an argument when my phone pings from my dresser. I step into my room and find an unknown number on the screen. Sara's been having problems with her phone, so I assume it's her.

"Hey," I say, hoping she's calling with good news. *Finally, something to cheer me up.*

No one replies from the other end of the line.

"Hello?"

Still nothing.

"Is someone there?" I ask, growing annoyed. Light breathing is all I hear. The idea that my sister is actually calling me hits me hard. I swallow, taking a seat on the edge of my bed.

"Alexis?" I ask, saying her name out loud after years of keeping her name to myself. "If it's you, you can—"

The line goes dead before I can finish.

I lie back onto my bed and take a breath. Do I still want the whole family reconnection or am I ready to give up? If she can't even talk to me on the phone, assuming that was her, what makes me think she's actually coming to Wind Valley?

Before I can change my mind, I make a choice. My sister knows where I live and how to get ahold of me. If she wants to see me, she'll find a way; I'm not going out of my way anymore trying to make it happen.

I toss the phone onto my bed before heading for the bathroom. Either I just made the best choice I could make or a dumb one.

"Logan, Ethan and I are going out for some beers and to play a few rounds of darts tonight, you in?' Conner says, poking his head into the bathroom while I brush my teeth. I nod and spit.

"Yes." A drink is exactly what I need.

I head back to my room to change and call Sara. The phone rings and goes to voicemail. First she cancels without much of an explanation and now she isn't answering her phone.

I really need that drink.

CHAPTER FIFTEEN

Sara

"When was the last time you went out anyway?" Liam asks me from behind the bar. I thought we got off this damn subject this morning. He sets the tray of new glassware on the counter and waits for my answer. I shrug and look away.

"I don't see why that would matter on the type of music we play." I say, since that was the conversation topic.

"It matters because I think you have been way too focused on getting this place up and running. You're missing out on the part where you should still have a life. Logan's doing it, why can't you and … I mean, why are you in such a hurry?"

I pin him with a glare. He knows damn well why I want this place to open as soon as it can. He holds his hands up in surrender style and takes a step back.

"Okay, okay so I know the answer to that, but come on, Sara. Last weekend didn't seem to be out of the ordinary for him. Do you think Logan is sitting at home every night watching reruns on the tube? No, he's probably out with his buddies."

I grunt and then laugh. Logan is a social guy, but going out isn't his thing.

"Seeing as how his best friend is married with a kid, I doubt Logan is doing a whole lot of going out. The other weekend was probably an exception to not make you sit at home with him," I argue.

"I'm not so sure. He works in a bar, and I bet he has more than just one friend. I've met him, remember—he's a people person. Besides, didn't your friend's brother move back? He's single, right? I bet he likes to go out."

Would Logan really start going out now that Conner's back? They grew up together and have always been friends. Logan was one of the few who actually kept in touch with Conner when no one else knew where he was. What if Conner wants to hit on girls? What if he needs a wing man? Nah, Logan isn't like that—he wouldn't do that to me.

"I trust him."

"Well, hey, my roommate Austin—who also happens to be in a band—he and his band members like to practice in our apartment. Usually when they're finished around ten or so, they invite a bunch of people over and we make it into a thing."

"You have parties at your place every weekend?" I ask him. That sounds crazy.

"Not every weekend, just, you know, three out of four a month maybe." He crosses his arms and grins at me. "Just come. I swear you will have fun and there will be other girls there. Some you'll even notice you have a lot in common with. You've been here for what, a month and a half now—have you even made any friends?"

"Yes, I have," I say quickly.

"Besides me." His eyebrows rise as he waits for my answer. I let out a sigh that halfway sounds like a groan.

"Fine, okay, so I haven't been going out since I've been here. There isn't anything wrong with that."

"No, but if you aren't going to take my word for it, then what about getting out there to learn the types of things this town is into? If you want this place to be successful, you should look at all your options."

I hate that he's right. I just wish there was another way I could go about it.

Defeated, I nod in his direction.

"Okay, when is this party of yours starting?" I ask. I should probably make myself somewhat decent before I go into the public. Liam looks at his watch and claps his hands together.

"Well, it's almost ten so now is a great time to stop working and start a party." He reaches for his back pocket and pulls out his phone. I push back my chair and stand to grab my coat while he quickly types something out and puts his phone back in his pocket. Hopefully, my agreeing to go out tonight will make up for the fact I have kept him here later than usual all week.

"Ready?" Liam asks. His eyes beam with excitement. He does the male version of a skip around the bar and doesn't stop until he is in front of me. He extends his arm.

"Shall we?"

I smile at the happiness on his face. Logan always knows when I am upset or starting to stress out and will do anything to cheer me up. I can't help but think that Liam and Logan are more alike each day. Wrapping my fingers in the crook of his arms, I nod.

"Yes we shall, but I need to stop by my place to freshen up," I say as we head for the door. "Should I meet you there?"

"Nonsense, it's getting dark out. I'll walk you to your place and wait for you. Then we can head over to my place. There's no way I would let a girl who looks like you wander anyplace alone downtown. Nice neighborhood or not, I don't trust a lot of people," he says.

I lock the door and relax. I might not know Liam very well, but he is becoming someone I truly enjoy being around. Maybe in another world we knew each other as more than coworkers. I ponder that thought, and right as we turn the corner to my apartment, it hits me. I'm about to be alone in my apartment with a guy. A guy who isn't Logan.

Logan

I hit send for the second time since we got to the BA. It isn't like Sara to ignore my calls, but I know better than anyone that if it goes straight to voicemail after a couple rings, someone hit the decline button. And it's been doing that all day.

"Dude, what are you doing?" Conner asks as he pulls the darts out of the dartboard. He stops next to the round high-top table where I am sitting and takes a swig of his beer. Ethan left us an hour ago, and I've apparently been poor company since that moment.

"You're acting like a total chick right now."

"I'm not acting like a girl," I say, placing my phone on the table and pushing it away from me.

"Refreshing the screen on your phone every two minutes is 100 percent girl behavior." Conner faces the dartboard once again and positions his foot as far on the yellow tape on the floor as he can without going over. His body straightens as he holds the dart in front of his face to focus on the bull's-eye ahead of him. The hand with the dart twitches like he is going to let go, but he doesn't. Letting his arm drop, he turns back to me.

"Let's make a wager, shall we?" A smug grin takes over his face. Everyone in Wind Valley is aware of Conner Brian and his wagers. In high school, he was known to never lose. Unless I feel like streaking, getting blackout drunk to the point I get an embarrassing tattoo of a lovebird on my bicep, or losing a shit ton of money, I should steer clear of anything involving Conner and a wager. I've learned my lesson—a few times.

"No," I say before he continues. I stand, grabbing the dart out of his hand and taking his spot behind the line. One more great reminder of why I should say no after losing three times in a row. Ethan and I are convinced Conner cheats, and that's after we deliberately set the tape farther back than it should be. Somehow, he still manages to win. Conner flops into a chair at the table and crosses his ankles.

"You can't say no when you don't even know what the wager is," he says in his best I-know-you're-interested tone. I shake my head and focus on the dartboard.

"I think—"

The first dart flees through the air. *Damn, way off.* I get ready to shoot the next one.

"Hey, are you listening to me?" Conner asks.

"Nope," I say, letting the second dart loose. *Damn, off again.*

"Well, shit—maybe you shouldn't bet against me. You're not playing so hot tonight." He laughs. "Is your game off because of Sara?" His tone is prying, but I ignore him.

"Are you two having a fight?"

I still don't answer and try to keep my focus on the dartboard.

"Is this a situation where she's mad and you have no idea why?"

Ignoring him is starting to get difficult. I pull my arms back, ready to let the third dart go.

"Is she with Liam?"

Fuck!

The dart goes fast from my hand and flops to the ground after hitting the board. In two steps I'm in Conner's face, and he doesn't even flinch.

"Shut the fuck up. She isn't with Liam. I'm so tired of everyone talking about Sara and Liam. She isn't with anyone but me," I say. My blood is boiling and my fists are clenched. If he knows what's good for him, he won't breathe Liam's name around me again. If he does, it better not be in the same sentence as Sara.

"Okay, jeez, man," he says, pushing me out of his space. "I'm trying to be the supportive friend here. All I'm asking is, are you letting her go or are we going to jump in the car, drive to Rockland, and kick some ass to get your girl back?"

My breathing picks up as his words play in my head. *Get your girl back.* I hadn't even realized I lost her, but maybe I slowly am. I grab my phone off the table and hit redial. With the phone to my ear I walk away from Conner. If she finally answers, I sure as hell don't want him around to hear our conversation.

This time, when the call makes it past the second ring, my body relaxes. She didn't ignore me. When the next ring cuts off halfway through, my heart starts to race.

"Hey, you." Sara's sweet voice fills my head. "I thought you would never call."

Never call? She can't be serious. Before I can reply to her, her voice is replaced with loud music and people yelling. I hear some scream Sara's name in the background and then *his* voice comes in loud and clear through the phone. *Is she drinking?*

"Hey to you, too," I say, attempting to keep my voice calm and pretend I didn't just hear him ask her to dance. "I actually did try calling you earlier, but it went to voicemail."

"You did?" she asks, followed by a giggle I've never heard before. "Stop it! I'm on the phone!" she yells and I flinch. What the fuck is going on over there? "Logan, can I call you back in two minutes? I need to get outside where I can hear you better."

"Yeah, sure thing," I say and hit the end button before she can say anything else. "Conner!" I yell over my shoulder as I start for the door. "That road trip is starting now!"

I don't know what I'm going to do when I get there or what I'm going to say, but I do know I'm not letting her go. Not today.

CHAPTER SIXTEEN

Sara

I stumble out of the sliding door to the backyard of Liam and Austin's townhouse for the fourth time—I think. There's a reason I keep coming out here—I just don't remember what it is.

For the last three hours I've done nothing but drink— moderately of course—dance, and meet a whole world of people I didn't know were out here. I wasn't planning on drinking, but then someone gave me a glass of moscoto and it's so good, I just keep drinking it.

Kate, one of the vocalists for Austin's band, likes Taylor Swift just as much as I do, even though she doesn't sing the same music. She also prefers to read and watch movies over hanging out at a party. The only reason she's here tonight is because Liam asked Austin to invite her for my sake. Sage, the other girl I met, is a definite groupie, but still we have a lot of the same interests as well. We even made plans to do a little shopping tomorrow after we have lunch. I didn't realize how lonely I actually felt until she invited me.

"Hey, is everything okay?" I turn at the sound of Liam's voice.

"Yeah, it was getting a little too hot in there for me. I just came out for some air."

"Alright." He shrugs. "Find me if you need anything."

I give a slight nod and then rest my arms on the porch railing. This place isn't so bad. The mountains are beautiful and everything is green. I love knowing I can walk outside and my chances of seeing wildlife are pretty high. My chances are the same in Wind Valley. Living here wouldn't be much different.

I jolt at the sound of a door slamming behind me and peek through the sliding doors to watch the commotion. Two guys are shoving each other while another keeps trying to stand between them. A girl screams and when everyone stops moving, I clasp my hand over my mouth. *Logan.* No, it can't be. Crap, I never called him back. How much have I had to drink? And how long has it been since I talked to him? I didn't drink that much, did I? Oh, I am going to have one bad hangover in the morning if I'm already envisioning Logan. I should call him. I miss him. Where's my phone?

"Where the fuck is she?"

Oh my god. I'm not imaging him. Logan *is* here. In Colorado. Crap! He's at Liam's apartment, looking for me. And since I can hear him through closed doors … he sounds pretty damn mad. Oh no, did something happen at the BA? To Kelsey or the baby?

"Dude, you're not going anywhere near her with that attitude."

"If you don't tell me where my girlfriend is, I swear you

will wish you had never met me by the time I am done pounding your face in."

"Logan." Everyone around us freezes at the shock in my voice. "What are you doing here?"

"I tried calling, but you didn't answer."

"I have no idea where my phone is," I say, giggling and taking a step toward him. "I lost it somewhere between the last time I talked to you and the time I made it out here."

I trip myself and fall into Logan's chest. Liam reaches out to steady me, but Logan shoves him back with the hand that isn't holding me up.

"Don't touch her," he says. *He's pissed.* "I think you've done enough already."

"Logan, stop. It's not Liam's fault. Actually, it's the opposite. He's been helping me relax with everything that been going on. I just needed one night when I didn't have to think about where I'm supposed to be or what I'm supposed to be doing."

"I should be the one you come to for those things, Sara."

"Hey, how do you know where Liam lives, and you can't be here for everything, Logan. You're a whole state away. Sometimes I need someone who is wherever I am to lean on."

"So call me next time. It's as easy as that."

I push out of his arms, but fall back into them. I can hold myself up just fine, I just don't want to because letting someone else do it right now—well, and that sounds a lot easier than doing it myself.

"I don't know why you're making this such a huge deal," I say, stepping away from him. "Do you not trust me to go out every now and then?"

"I trust you perfectly," he says, turning his attention to Liam. "It's the people around you I'm not so sure of."

"Who, Liam?" I say and then burst into laughter before I can stop myself. "It's Liam, Logan. What in the world do you have to be afraid of? That I'm going to let him move in with me and not tell you!"

"This is exactly what I mean. He's telling you shit and he doesn't even know the whole story."

"Well, he knows enough to tell me about it. And it's been an entire week! A week, Logan. Plenty of time for you to tell me."

"I know." His voice drops and that's when I notice the audience our argument has captured. I glance around at all the faces. A few of them are my new employees, which sparks my embarrassment. I shouldn't be here. Not just because of Logan and what it's doing to him, but because these people work for me. I can't be both a friend and boss here.

"I have to go," I say to Liam.

"I'll drive you," he says, moving toward me.

I nod.

"I'll take her," Logan cuts in.

"Logan, it's—"

"No, you're my girlfriend. I will take you home."

The moment the words leave his mouth, my heart drops into my stomach. My eyes go wide and I just stare at him.

"God, Logan, don't be so intense. Being my boyfriend doesn't mean you get to make choices for me!" I yell and run through the house. This isn't my finest hour. And it's one of the biggest reason I never drink. I don't like the person I become, and no matter how hard I try, I can never control myself. The front door slams behind me just after I hear Logan shout my name.

No way in hell am I letting a man I'm supposed to be in a relationship with—meaning we're a team—think he gets to make my decisions for me. It may be the wine talking, but if this is what it takes to be with someone I care about, I'm not so sure it's worth it.

Logan

"You can't just act like a crazy person!" Sara yells once I've caught up with her. She's walking down the street, and she isn't slowing down.

"The fuck I can't! I haven't heard from you, and when I finally make it down here, you're out partying and drinking, which you never do by the way, so that's awesome. You feel more comfortable drinking around some guy you just met than you do around me. That makes me feel real good."

"Stop it, Logan. It wasn't like that and you know it. Liam invited me because the bar has been stressing me out. He saw that I needed to relax."

"Relax, yeah, I'm sure that is exactly what he was going to help you do later tonight."

"Logan, jealousy doesn't look good on you. Whatever you have going on in your mind, you need stop it and chill out. Liam and I are just friends. How many times do I have to tell you this?"

"A couple more. Maybe until I never see you in his apartment again or in his line of sight."

"Before I left, you told me to have trust, Logan, and I did. What about you? Where is your trust in me?"

"I trust you, Sara, I just told you this five minutes ago. It's him I don't trust."

"You're going to have to start. He's going to be working with us for a while. I mean, I'm still not sure when I'm going to make it back to Wyoming."

Everything inside me is on high alert.

"This is a joke, right? I thought there were only a few more weeks."

"There are, but—"

"But you want to stay here, with Liam."

"That's not even it. I want to be here for the Silver Tap. I wasn't there in the beginning of the BA. I didn't get to watch it grow and succeed. I can do that here. I want to take pride in this place before I leave some guy in charge of it."

The way she says *some guy* makes me feel a bit better.

"I trust Liam more than I should, but I still—"

"Whoa, you trust him? After a couple weeks?"

"Well, yeah, I—"

"It took me years, Sara. *Years* before you wanted to be alone with me. You never even chose me to run the BA, your father did. Send Liam to the BA, and I'll stay here with you."

She stops and my hands find her shoulders. I rub my thumbs over her bare skin. I want her to nod her head and smile and agree with me.

"I can't do that to him, Logan. His life is here."

"You can't do it even for us?"

"That's not a fair choice to make."

"Sounds fair enough to me. Either you want me here, or you don't."

Sara looks up and a tear slips from her eye. She walks away again, turning a corner until we arrive at my truck. I open the door for her and once she's buckled in, I glance back to see Conner trailing behind us at a good distance. I take my time walking to the driver's side and we sit in silence until Conner gets in. Even then, no one talks until we're at Sara's apartment. Conner stays in the truck while I walk Sara to the door. She still doesn't say anything after she unlocks the door. She sets her purse and keys down on the counter and looks at me. She shrugs. *What the fuck do I do with that?* Before I can make up my mind, she turns for her bedroom. I take that as I sign I should go, even though every part of me wants to stay.

"Logan, stop. You can't just leave. We need to talk this out," she says, now standing in the doorway of her room.

"Talk? You haven't spoken in the last thirty minutes. How much longer do I have to wait? Your silence isn't fair to me, and the fact you can't tell me you want us more that you want the Silver Tap … well, it doesn't look good in my eyes," I say, praying she starts talking now. But she doesn't. "Call me when you know what you want."

"We can't fight like this. This isn't us."

"I know, I just … the thought of losing you terrifies me," I say, pausing to give her one last chance to talk to me. When her response is to look away, I turn for the door and it takes everything I have to hold my head high and not turn around to go back to her. If she doesn't want me, I'm not going to bust my ass trying to change her mind. We've been at this long enough she should know what she wants by now.

Clearly, it isn't me.

CHAPTER SEVENTEEN

Sara

I can't believe Logan came down here acting like a caveman. The way he treated Liam at the party, like every word was a warning. He wanted people to know I was his, and I want that, too. Every time Logan acts that way, I can't resist him. But tonight was different. Something different in his eyes —I can't determine what it was exactly, but someone once told me that fear can make a person mad. And the look I saw tonight … I'm almost positive it was screaming fear all over.

As much as I'm scared of what made him feel this way, I'm even more angry that I need to talk to someone about what happened tonight and that someone should be him, but I can't because he's right. Something has changed since I've been here. I'm not sure Wyoming is the place for me anymore. There is only one other person I can even consider calling right now. I scramble to my couch where I dig through my purse. It's late and I'll probably wake the baby, but I'm calling Kelsey anyway.

"Sara, what's wrong?" she answers after one ring.

"Logan showed up here tonight," I blurt out. I'm too worked up to ease into the conversation. I hear the baby crying in the background, and I know Kelsey will understand that it's best to just cut to the chase. "He came here for me and I wasn't here."

"Where were you?"

"At Liam's."

"Liam's, like his apartment?"

"Yes."

"Alone?"

"No! Oh, wow, no. His roommate was having a party and he invited me."

"Well that was nice of him. I bet you needed a break."

"Exactly, but all Logan saw was me choosing to relax with Liam and not him, then he asked me to send Liam to Wyoming so he could come here to Colorado with me and I said no."

"What? Why would you say no? Does this mean you and Logan aren't dating anymore?"

"I don't know. I just panicked and blurted out something about liking Rockland in a different way than Wind Valley. And then he stormed off and told me to call him when I got my life together."

"You like Colorado better?"

"No, I just … he was all weird with Liam, and said something to make it sound like he owned me or something. Maybe I'm just overreacting."

"Oh, that's intense, but jealousy makes people do things they never thought they would."

"Yeah," I say. Kelsey isn't helping as much as I thought she would.

"Do you want to hear a secret? It's probably going to make you feel like shit, but it will explain a lot."

"Oh no, what is it?"

"Well, Ethan told me Logan has been looking into finding his sister. Last I heard, it wasn't going well."

"He is?" My heart breaks thinking of how this conversation has never come up.

"Yeah, it's insane. I can't imagine not knowing my real family."

"I have to go." I tap the end button and lean back on the couch. That was the fear I saw. The fear of his real family not wanting him. I've always thought of Logan as family, and I should have chosen him, I know I should have, but I didn't and now he probably thinks no one wants him. If only he knew how wrong he is.

Logan

"You want to talk about it?" Conner asks after we've been driving for a while.

"No."

"You're positive? Because we have another two hours to drive and as much as I like heavy music, I'd prefer to show up at home without my ears bleeding."

"She just—"

"Keep going."

"I don't—"

"You almost have it."

"She didn't pick me," I spit out.

Silence is the only response I get.

"Hey, man, you wanted me to talk, and now you have nothing to say."

"Well, fuck, I didn't say I was going to know what to say back to you." Conner grunts.

"Well, think of something. I'm tired of no one having anything to say to me."

I hit the steering wheel with my palm. *Fuck.* She couldn't even pick me. Before she left, she wanted to be with me, and now she can't even make a decision.

"Alright, so, I know this whole road trip was my idea, but I have to be honest. I thought you would act a bit more smooth when we got there," Conner says, keeping his eyes on his phone.

"Smooth? I was way fucking smooth."

"Yeah, I'm not sure about that. You acted like you were back in high school or even junior high. Sara had an excuse because she'd been drinking, but I don't see one for you. And I know exactly why you were there, so to me it wasn't anything out of the ordinary, but to others you may have come off as a bit more intense."

I glare at him. "Intense?"

"Yeah, you were kind of scary."

I let his words soak in. I wasn't that bad. It's not like I went in their throwing fists and handing out black eyes. I couldn't have scared anyone. Did I? Shit. What if I scared Sara and that's the reason she didn't answer me?

"And not to mention—"

"Okay, I think we've done enough talking," I interrupt him before he can say anything else to make me feel like a jackass.

Intense.

Sara used that same word at Liam's apartment. Maybe I am intense, but it's only because I care about her. And maybe I need to tone it down a notch, but no one ever said love needed to be monitored. Now is not the time to start either.

CHAPTER EIGHTEEN

Sara

"I knew he would do something like this," my father says over the phone.

"No, you didn't,"

"Yes, I did. I had a feeling he was a little on the crazy side."

"He's not crazy. He's mad and I hurt him."

"Mad and hurt turns people crazy."

I roll my eyes and plop onto the sofa. My plan had been to not tell my father about Logan, but somehow he overheard someone at the BA and now here we are.

"I don't think you should see him right now." My father's voice is firm.

"I can't do that. I may be mad, too, but eventually we are going to have to talk this out."

"Just stay in Colorado for a couple weeks. Liam can keep you company in the meantime. Now that's the kind of boy you should end up with."

"Dad, stop. I don't like Liam, not that way."

"And why not?"

"Are we really having this conversation?"

"You spend more time with him, and he has a solid head on his shoulders."

"He lives here. I didn't plan to be around him more. It's just the way it happened. He's the assistant in a bar, Dad. Let's not go giving out awards just yet."

"All I'm saying is that you spend more time with him than you do Logan, and I think there is a reason for that."

"Yeah, because you always schedule for Liam to go to Wind Valley and not me. You have it planned perfectly to keep us apart. If anyone is to blame right now, it's you for keeping us apart."

"I've done no such thing. If Logan wants to be with you, he wouldn't care what I tell him to do."

I sigh into the phone, hoping the noise alone will the get the point across that I am done with this conversation.

"Dad, I have to go now."

I hang up the phone before he can reply and dial Logan's number immediately. The only way we are going to fix this is if we talk about it. It's already been two days and, as unpleasant as this conversation is going to be, we need to have it.

"Hello?" a female's voice answers Logan's phone.

"Um, hi, is Logan around?"

Who's answering his phone?

"Uh, he's busy right now," she says, and when she giggles, the noise goes right through my ear and crunches my heart.

Abby.

That bitch.

I end the call, storming out of my apartment. I need a distraction and leaving my phone—the one I had to buy because I couldn't find my old one—on the couch is a perfect one. For someone who thinks responsibility is important, I can't seem to keep a cell phone longer than a couple of months.

I head out the door and straight for the Silver Tap, because really, where else am I going to go?

Throwing the door open, I'm shocked to find Liam there. He's behind the counter and has almost the entire back wall marked with labels of where everything should go. I stand there, frozen. He glances behind him, giving me a sad smile.

"Another idea of Logan's," he says quietly and shrugs.

I sigh, completely defeated by my life right now. I'm too young for this. Knowing your future should be easier than this.

"So, hey, I know what's going on by the look on your face, and I think I should tell you something. If you hate me when I'm done and want to fire me, I'll fully understand," he says.

I raise one eyebrow as he piques my interest. I wait, but he doesn't say anything right away.

"Well?" I ask. Why can't anyone I know communicate like a normal, person anymore?

"When I was in Wind Valley last weekend, your father invited me over for dinner."

I roll my eyes. *Of course he did.*

"During dinner he made a comment about how he's extremely proud of you and everything you've done down here, but he is worried about you." Liam takes a cautious step toward me. His eyes don't leave mine. "He suggested that I invite you out because no one visits and all your friends back home are still having fun. He was afraid he was taking that away from you. I didn't think anything of it at the time."

I sniffle and blink back the tears. I know exactly what happened.

"I swear I thought it was innocent. Even when he made the comment about how disappointed he was that certain people weren't making the effort to see you. I never put two and two together. Not until you did come out and Logan showed up, and now you're—I don't even know what you are."

"We're on a break, you could say," I whisper.

"I never realized how much your dad was pushing this."

"I did," I say.

"You knew?" Liam looks at me with confusion.

I nod. A tear slips and I wipe it away. I should have never let go of that hunch so easily.

"Well, that's great!" Liam says with excitement. "Then it was all your dad and had nothing to do with you and Logan. You can end your break now."

"No, we can't." Another sniffle. "Knowing this makes it worse. It means I didn't trust Logan. It means that my father knew how to play us against each other and we weren't strong enough to get through it. We should be strong. I should have known. Now everything is a mess, and I don't know how to fix it."

My shoulders shake as I cry. Liam steps around the bar, hugging me awkwardly.

"It's going to be okay. Breakups suck, but eventually you move on."

I take a breath, releasing it slowly when he says "breakup."

Returning to his spot behind the bar, Liam watches me with concern.

"I don't know what to say, but I think everything will work out. Just give it time."

Biting my bottom lip, I nod and get up. I thought being away from my apartment would help, but anything is better than having to talk about it. Being alone is exactly what I need.

Logan

Clara looks up at me with her big, brown eyes and another bubble of spit forms on her lips. Her legs twitch, landing stick straight before she curls back up and a smile appears. Then she spits up all over me. It's nasty, but I laugh anyway.

"Here, take this." Ethan hands me the spit-up towel from Clara's baby bag. Kelsey laughs and Abby joins her. A flash in her hand reminds me that I asked her to answer my phone because I was too busy playing with Clara.

"Who was it?" I ask. Kelsey pulls Clara out of my arms and the spit starts to run down my shirt. *Gross.*

Abby's smile drops, she shrugs, and looks away. "I think it was Sara, but I didn't recognize the number."

My head jerks up and I push off the couch toward her.

"Why didn't you get me?" I grab my phone off the counter and look up in time to find Ethan whispering something to Kelsey. They both freeze when they catch me looking.

"What number is she calling from?"

They shrug in unison. *Right, they have no idea.*

I hit redial and head down the hall to my bedroom. I don't want to have this conversation in front of anyone. There's going to be a lot of groveling on my side, and they don't need to witness it. The ringing ends and her voicemail picks up.

"It's Sara, leave a message."

"Hey, it's me. Call me."

I sit on the edge of my bed and wait. The memory of when I broke up with her high school comes to mind. I'd left her house and went straight to the field looking for a fight. I found one, took out some stress, and went home to call Sara and tell her I was wrong. I left her a voicemail then, too, asking her to call me back. She never did.

Twenty minutes later, I call her again. Abby answering my phone was a bad idea. I seem to be having a lot of those lately, and I need to get it together. The call goes to voicemail again. This time I don't leave a message. I just hang up and pray things are different and this time, she will call me back.

CHAPTER NINETEEN

Sara

Four hours is how long it takes me to drive back to Wind Valley. I don't want to be here right now. One week isn't long enough and I need more time to think, but I want more than anything to be in town with Kelsey on her repeated biggest day ever. Facing Logan at the reception is a small price to pay. My fear now is that I'll see him before I've completely decided what I'm going to say. I've thought about it all day every day, more on the drive, and even more since I checked into the hotel where Kelsey and I are getting ready, but I still got nothing.

The bathroom door to the suite Kelsey and I are in opens slowly as she steps out. A smile takes over her face as she holds out her arms.

"You look freaking amazing," I say, touching a strand of her hair. She colored it a shade darker today, got a spray tan, and is now ready to go in a white and gold sheath dress with sparkling gold heels.

"You don't think it's too much?" she asks, glancing at herself in the mirror.

We make eye contact through our reflections, and even though my heart is breaking inside for Logan and me, it has room to be happy for Kelsey and Ethan.

"I think you look perfect. Ethan has no clue how good he has it." I force a smile and start to fidget with my hair. Everyone is waiting for Kelsey and Ethan to show up downstairs. Which means for me, I'll need to head down before her, and even though I'll be in a room full of people I've known for years, I don't want to have to make small talk with any of them.

I'm only twenty-three. I still have my whole life ahead of me. A whole life to make bad choices, make mistakes, and get to know people outside of Wind Valley. Yeah, so I've been to more countries than most people my age, but that was all from being spoiled by my father's money.

"I still have you and Logan sitting next to each other. Is that okay?" Kelsey asks, and there's no mistaking the concern etched in her voice. I look away and grab some gloss.

"I honestly thought you two would be talking again by now." She frowns.

Me too.

"Yeah, of course. It's completely okay." I pop my lips together. I don't want to think about Logan just yet. "Are we ready to go?"

Right as Kelsey opens her lips to answer, a crazy concocted knock at the door stops her. We smile. That's the knock she told Ethan to use. I give her a quick hug and head for the door, laughing at the disappointment Ethan's face takes on when I step out of the room.

"She's coming, lover boy. Hold your pants," I say, patting him on the shoulder and continuing on my way.

The reception room is huge with white, red, and gold all over. People are everywhere, sitting, eating, and drinking. The music hasn't started, but the chatter in the room fills the silence in my head. I glance around, searching for my parents or anyone else I may want to avoid. I don't need any surprises. If I spot Logan first, then I will always know where he's at, and from there, I can successfully avoid him at all points during the night. If I time it right, I can get through dinner putting up with a maximum of only ten minutes of awkward talking time.

Abby's annoying laughter catches my attention from across the room. I glare at her and then immediately feel guilty. Technically, there's no proof she and Logan are anything more than friends. Just because she answered his phone and is still living in his apartment doesn't mean anything. *I hope.*

Abby's my friend and she has been since we were kids, but she was also Kelsey's friend back when she fooled around with Tyler, Kelsey's ex-boyfriend. The woman has got to know that even though we're friends, a part of me doesn't trust her with Logan. Yet she's still always around him, and I'm always questioning why I'm still friends with her.

My eyes remain focused on her as she talks to a group of people I recognize but can't quite name when Logan walks up behind her. Abby smiles at him and then pops her hip out, giving him a pouty face. She adjusts his tie, he smiles at her, and then she straightens his coat before winking at him and walking away.

That sure looks like some damn couple behavior to me.

.   .   .

Logan

"Logan, seriously, Sara isn't going to fall head over heels for you all over again if you walk in there with a crooked tie and a wrinkled jacket," Abby says, straightening my tie. "And would it kill you put a freaking smile on your face? We all know you're sad, but nobody died and it's time you start to act normal again."

She does a poor attempt to remove the wrinkles on my coat. I flash her my best smile, maybe a bit of an exaggerated one, to show her I'm trying.

"Ugh, whatever. That will have to do. Now get out of here and go find her before she catches you standing here and assumes the worst."

"No shit," I say, my eyes widening when I realize I said it out load.

Abby winks at me. "Just don't mess it up this time."

Trust me, no one wants to make this work out more than I do. The group Abby had been talking to slowly moves away from me. I stuff my hands into my pants pockets and my gut practically lunges into my throat when I see Sara watching me from across the room. Her eyes are big and beautiful but filled with sadness. There's no doubt in my mind that I put that glazed expression on her face just now.

Never taking my eyes off of her, I take a step in her direction. She shakes her head and I stop. Then she walks away.

"Well, I'd say you're off to fabulous start. Don't you think?"

I groan, rubbing the back of my neck at Conner's words.

"Yeah, man, real winner right here."

"I'm just going to toss this out here, but I'm starting to pick up on the fact you and Sara have communication issues. It looks like you two can't even make it through 'a look' without getting the wrong impression. And just now, you did exactly what she wanted. You stopped after she told you 'no.' We both know she assumes something is going on between you and Abby. We both *also* know that's not the case, but instead of talking about it, you two just let the situation get worse."

Who'd have expected that much wisdom from Conner? It's so deep, I have to pause and let it soak in, especially the part about how I'm making this worse. Nah, I'm not doing that. It's no secret Sara and I have never mastered this communication thing. He takes a swing of the beer in his hand.

"That's your fucking cue, man. Follow her and don't take no for an answer until she talks to you. Either that or end it." His raises his left brow as he pushes me forward.

"Fuck, okay. I know what I need to do, but I also know Sara."

"Yeah, you knew single my-career-is-my-life Sara Connelly." His voice gets lower. "This is I-found-love-in-a-relationship Sara Connelly. New woman. Now go resolve this mess you're in."

Just hearing her name puts a smile on my lips. I don't think twice. I turn and head straight for Sara. Unfortunately for me, she isn't in the same spot she was a moment ago. Now, she's in front of the drink table with Beth and she's standing next to Abby.

I walk a little faster, hoping Abby doesn't make things worse.

<h1 style="text-align:center">CHAPTER TWENTY</h1>

Sara

"Logan is such an amazing guy."

I'm about ready to vomit right here in front of everyone. I can't even tell if Abby is talking in a I-love-him way or in a you-need-to-know-what-you're-missing way.

"He's funny and cute and smart and—"

"She knows," Beth interrupts her, and I hold back the cheer that is dying to slip from my lips. Thank god she said something, because if it had been me, it wouldn't have come out so polite.

"Does she, Beth?" Abby snaps. "Because if you ask me, she's being selfish and acting like a child."

What the—?

"Oh, she's acting like a child? This coming from you? Really, Abby."

"I'm not perfect, I know this. But come on, what Sara's putting Logan through is just bullshit, and she needs to get her shit together before he leaves her for someone else."

Beth narrows her eyes at Abby and steps forward. It's like I'm not even here.

"Oh, and who *is* he supposed to end up with, huh? Who's he going to pick—someone like you?" Beth's voice is quiet but still full of attitude. At this point, I'd be less afraid if she were yelling.

"Well, I'm paying more attention to him these days than her, so yeah, someone who treats him better, like me, would be a great choice."

This time, I speak up before Beth can defend me again.

"Living with him has only allowed you to see one side of the story, Abby. So unless you play a bigger role in the fact we aren't speaking, I think it's best if you just stop talking about it," I say. I sound way more calm than how I'd planned for that to come out.

"I'm just trying to make you see—"

"I see just fine, Abby. And what I see between the two of you doesn't look good." I turn to leave because Kelsey and Ethan don't deserve a scene like this today. But I just can't resist a peek over my shoulder. "And if you really are trying to help him, you should probably stop touching him so much. It isn't helping him or you at all."

I start to walk away before I've fully turned back around and I smack right into a chest— Logan's chest. My breathing picks up immediately and I swallow, pushing my lips together before I say something I don't mean. And maybe also because I miss him and from the way he's looking at me right now, smiling is what I really want to do.

I watch as his throat bobs while he looks me over. We haven't been this close to each other in more than a week, not counting the night he showed up at Liam's apartment. We were too busy fighting then to enjoy the fact we were together.

When neither of us makes the motion to leave, Logan pins his eyes on mine.

"Would you two mind giving us a minute?" he says.

Beth and Abby walk past us without even a word or a glance. I break our eye contact, hoping to find someone who will call my attention, giving me an excuse to walk away right now. I could just do it—leave. But deep down I miss Logan and want to be near him. That's the exact reason this whole situation hurts so badly. I want him more than I could ever imagine, but I don't know if our being together is right for me anymore.

"Can we go somewhere to talk?" My body absorbs his deep, smooth voice, and before I know it, my head is bobbing and he's taking my hand in his. I hear a few whispers as we walk through the crowd, but I keep my head down so I don't have to see their faces. Logan leads us to a patio outside. The warm summer air hits my skin, relaxing me.

"I'm so sorry. For everything," he says quickly, taking my hand. "For not trusting you, for not giving Liam a chance, for driving down there and acting like a total jackass. I was scared of losing you and because of that, I've done nothing but push you away. The last thing I want is for us to be where we are now. I want to make this work." He kisses my forehead and steps back to look me in the eyes. The pain I see in his makes me look away and take a deep breath.

"Logan, I accept your apology, but things are different now. I don't know if it's me or if we rushed into this—"

"Rushed it? Officially dating or not, we've been Sara and Logan for years. There's definitely no rushing."

"And right when things were great, we made a choice that we didn't think through." All hope falls from his face. That wasn't how I intended for that to come out.

"You regret being in a relationship with me?"

"No, I don't." I shake my head and press my lips together to keep the bottom one from shaking. *Don't cry, Sara, not yet.*

"Yes, you do. Have you heard what you just said? You think we rushed it and that we didn't make the right choice."

I take a few choked breaths before I answer.

"I never said it was the wrong choice, Logan. I just—"

"Well, if it's not the right one, then what is it?" His voice cracks. I wish he were mad right now. I could handle mad Logan, but heartbroken Logan eats me to pieces.

I sigh and drop into the wooden chair nearby. I'm not making any sense. If I don't even know what I want, how can I explain it to him?

"I'm sorry, Logan. I really am. But I need more time to think about everything. A lot is going on, and I thought the idea of you and me was going to be the easiest thing in my life, but it's not even close."

"I'll quit the bar."

"What?" My head snaps up. Logan's hands are on his hips as he stands in front of me nodding. He kneels and takes my hands in his.

"We're never going to make this work if we're in separate states. I'm quitting and moving to Colorado. One of us needs to make a choice, because if neither of us is willing to make sacrifices, then this is going to blow up in our face."

"So then, I'm the selfish one for not coming back? I don't want to be in a relationship where it looks like I'm putting in half the effort, just as I don't want to be in a relationship where I'm not even talking to my boyfriend."

Tears sting in the back of my eyes. I stand quickly and head for the doors before Logan sees them.

"That's it then? Just like that, you don't want to be together?"

"Jesus, Logan, is that what I said?"

"Sure as fuck sounded like it," he growls.

"I just need more time." I have a full on waterworks display going now. "I'll call you when I'm ready. I promise."

I let out a breath as I finally grab the door knob.

"Sara, wait," Logan whispers behind me. "I love you."

My heart crumbles.

"I love you, too," I say before stepping through the door and leaving without saying goodbye to anyone.

* * *

"So, how's life treating you?" Liam asks when I enter the bar the next Wednesday morning. Concern is written all over his face as he crosses his arms over his chest.

Dandy.

"Great," I tell him instead and walk right past him. I have been avoiding him all morning because every day when I get to work, he plays twenty questions, trying to get me to talk about Logan. I won't do it. I don't want to.

"Yeah, by the sarcastic tone in your voice, I don't believe you."

"Believe whatever you want, Liam. I'm the best I can be right now. My only focus now is on preparing this bar for the opening. Who knows? If everything goes well, I'll even stay here, in Colorado—permanently," I say more for dramatic effect than anything. The chances of my actually moving here are zero.

Andi, too, watches me with worried eyes as I move calmly to the office. Her lips twitch like she wants to say something, but instead, she looks away. Why does everyone want to talk about this? I can't even make up my own mind, and yet I'm supposed to know what to say when anyone asks about it.

I close the door and drop onto the sofa, resting my head against the back. Why don't I have one of these in Wyoming? I really need a couch in my office at the BA. I'm about five seconds into debating whether or not I want to make the call and order one when Liam bursts through the door.

"We need to talk." He walks right in and stands over me. All hints of concern are gone. He actually looks mad.

I groan. "Why does everyone keep saying this to me? I don't feel like talking to anyone. I just want to be me and live my life right now. I don't want to worry about what's going to happen between Logan and me. We didn't find a way to trust each other. Why is everyone missing this?"

"Stop, stop—I get it." He holds up his hand.

"You do?"

"Yeah, but I was just going to tell you that the tables and chairs finally arrived and, well, they aren't exactly what we ordered."

I spring from my spot on the sofa and push past him. Everything was going so smoothly. How can I be running into a mess right now? If things get held up now, I'll have to push the opening back and then I'll have to wait even longer to see Logan.

Ugh!

If I even want to. I have no idea what I'm doing. I should be mad about the furniture and fix this, but everything makes me think of Logan. That's the only thing I really want to fix.

I mentally shake any thought of him from my head. If he really wanted to fix things, he wouldn't wait for me to call him. The Logan I know would come right out and tell me I'm being stubborn. But he hasn't. I don't know who he is now or who I want to be. I can't think about this right now.

"Is the delivery guy still here?" I head for the door.

"He went to call his manager to find out what went wrong." Liam follows me out of the office. Andi and Brit—the other bartender slash waitress I hired—are sitting at the bar watching me, but the chairs aren't anywhere in this room. I jump when the office door slams behind me and turn around in time to see Liam locking it.

"What are you doing?"

"We can't let you keep hiding yourself away, Sara. You need to talk about this, get it out there, vent, or whatever it is girls do to de-stress. Andi and Brittany are here to listen. I'm sticking around to make sure you don't try to bolt."

"Bolt?" I huff. "Yes, I'm a bolter, so you better stick around." I throw my hands up. "This is insane—there isn't anything wrong with me."

"You're wearing two different flip-flops," Brittany speaks up.

"And you hair is frizzy, like maybe you didn't brush it today," Andi adds.

"I—" They can't be serious. Yeah, so I've been a little sluggish; this is normal twenty- something behavior. "I'm fine."

"No, you're not. Logan is—"

"Don't start with me," I interrupt Andi and take a deep breath and swallow. Just hearing his name shreds my heart into pieces. "I can't, okay. Please. Just don't." My chin drops to my chest as I silently pray they won't go on.

"You have to talk about him. If you don't, you'll never be able to fix this." Liam says from behind me. His hand gently touches my shoulder and I shrug away from him.

"If any of you knew me, actually knew me, you would know that this is what Logan and I do. We love and we fight. Over and over. Not once have we been able to make it work." Tears sting as my eyes and my lip quivers. "Being apart is what's best for us right now, and who knows, it might be the only thing that can salvage at least a friendship for us." The first tear flows down my cheek and the rest quickly follow. "I'm going to take the afternoon off. If the tables and chairs really do come in, I trust you can handle it."

Liam unlocks the office door and I step inside to grab my purse. I keep my head down as I pass the girls. I don't want people to see me cry. Especially those who should be acting more like my employees than my friends. I can't let them see me weak, but it's too late.

They just watched as my heart broke for Logan.

CHAPTER TWENTY-ONE

Logan

"Stop playing like such a jackass!" Ethan passes the ball to me with as much force as he can. It hits my chest and I grunt. Conner and Ethan stop to take a breath.

"Dude, what the fuck?" I shout at him. I tuck the ball under my arm and step toward him. Conner reaches out to stop me from taking another step.

"Serves you right, man," he says and pushes me back.

"You've be acting like a prick all afternoon, and you're taking it out on us and the game," Ethan pipes up from across the court.

I roll my eyes and move the ball to rest under my other arm. "You guys are acting like a bunch of babies because I can play basketball better than you. That's all this is."

"No, man, it's not just today." Ethan stares hard at me.

"Yeah, you've been in a mood since you and Sara split up. Don't you think it's time to call her and work this out? I can't stand watching you mope around the apartment and then go to work just to act like a dick there, too." This from Conner, who can't even have a civil conversation with his son's mother long enough to get an hour visit with him.

"She'll call when she's ready, and we didn't split up. It doesn't work like that," I snap back, throwing the ball at Ethan. I'm not in the mood to play anymore, and with the attitude they just brought out in me, it's probably best I stay away from people right now. I walk off the court and into the men's locker room. I stuff everything in my bag, sling it over my shoulder, and don't look back as I exit the gym. I toss my bag into the back of my truck.

Fuck. How much more space does she need? Why hasn't she called?

I slam the door once I'm inside and pull my phone from my pocket. I pull up Sara's number and my thumb hovers over the call button. All I have to do it tap it. One tap and I'm calling her and praying that she answers. I stare at the little green button, confused, angry, and hurt. She'll call. She always does.

I click out of her contact and to my main calls. This time, I stare long and hard at the number I believe Alexis called me from a couple weeks ago. Would she answer if I called it back? Putting effort into contacting her would distract me from waiting on Sara.

Sara or my sister?

Fuck.

That isn't even a question. I close out of my phone completely and toss it onto the passenger seat. If I had chosen Sara on her birthday, none of this would be happening right now.

· · ·

Sara

I step into the brightly lit bar and don't bother removing my sunglasses. No one wants to see my puffy red eyes, and my eyes don't want to see the light. There isn't anyone in view, which means if Liam and Andi are here, they're probably in the back room. As if I'm pulled by a magnet, I head straight for the office. Thank goodness I don't have to put up with any awkward interactions this morning. The other day was bad enough.

"Morning," Liam says, popping up from behind the bar.

"Jesus," I sputter, taking a step back and covering my heart with my hand. "What're you doing down there?"

He raises a broken glass. "I thought it would be cool if I had some awesome glass flipping move when we open." He shrugs. "Bad idea."

"Clearly," I reply in a less than friendly tone. He stares at me a minute before I continue toward the office.

"How was the reception, for real this time, Sara?" he asks, knowing exactly where I'm heading. "I didn't ask you about it more than once in the last two days, but today I figured why not? You've had a few days to cool down."

"It was fine." I don't turn around. I place my hand on the doorknob.

"Just fine?"

I ignore him. I don't want to talk about this. I twist the knob, but it stops. I twist again and jiggle it a bit. He locked it. *Again.*

I flip around, crossing my arms when I catch Liam with a smile on his face.

"I had a feeling you were going to try to shut everyone out today. Not happening."

"Nope, sure isn't," Andi adds, stepping into view from the storage room.

"This isn't funny. Unlock the door."

"No can do, boss," Liam says. "I may have misplaced the key."

"Liam, I swear to you, if you don't unlock that door for me right now, you will be demoted."

"Ouch." He laughs. "You're going to have to make a more serious threat than that. Helping fix whatever you have going on with your boyfriend, is worth losing my job."

"What am I missing?" Brit scowls at Liam.

"Nothing," I say, giving up quickly. I'm not in the mood to argue with anyone right now.

I pull up a seat at the bar and bury my face in my elbow. "If I stay out here can I at least not talk about my weekend?"

"What's that? I couldn't hear you." Andi laughs. "Oh, this came for you on Saturday. When are you changing your mailing address, by the way?"

I never changed it because I didn't plan on staying here long. Instead of answering her, I peek up to see what she has. A manila envelope sits in front of me.

There isn't a return address on it, but my name is written on it in the same handwriting I spent hours of high school staring at.

"Open it," she says.

I hesitate. Whatever's inside is more than likely not going to help me feel better. Opening this at home is the best idea.

Liam slides an envelope opener at me. *Looks like I'm opening this now.*

I take my frustration out on the opener and tear the top off. Then I give them both an "are you happy now?" smile.

On top is a note from Logan.

Sara,

Things are rough right now. I feel like my entire world is falling apart. That weekend when I was there, I was an idiot. I acted like a crazy, jealous boyfriend. I never want to act like that again.

There's no excuse for my behavior, but I think I realize how it came to be. I've been keeping something from you and I assumed you were doing the same. Finding my sister, Alexis, is something I've wanted for a while now. When I contacted the agency that placed us with our foster families, they couldn't give me any information. Tyler and his computer skills helped me get an address. I wrote to her including my phone number and address, asking her to come to Wind Valley. I chose your father's offer over you because I wanted to be here if she came. I chose finding my sister over you. That was the biggest mistake I've ever made.

We've never had the typical relationship. Even when we were just friends, you always meant more to me. I can't imagine a life without you. If friends is what you want, I'll do it, but I'm leaving the decision up to you.

I'll love you forever,
Logan

Tears fall uncontrolled down my face as I pull out the photos included with the letter. Photos from when we were younger up to my birthday last month. Dance photos, basketball games, barbeques, the lake, prom, and more. Logan has been a huge part of my life and, like him, I can't imagine my life without him in it.

Not even attempting to wipe the tears away, I excuse myself. How could we love each other the way we do and still act like this? I have to make a decision today. I'm either all in or all out; Logan deserves better than this.

Logan

It could be my newfound hate with the world that has made me stop caring, or I've been hiding the real Logan for a very long time. Right now, I hope it's the former. Otherwise, I'm a total jackass.

"She has to go," I tell Conner. He's sitting in the living room and I'm standing in the kitchen. He looks away from the TV for this conversation. Having someone's full attention is a good start to a tough topic.

"I know, but I feel bad. The only reason she's staying here in the first place is because she doesn't have anywhere else to go. If we kick her out, too, she could be homeless."

"I don't really care where she goes as long as it isn't anywhere in my apartment." I cross my arms over my chest. "Her living here is not working out."

"She didn't cause you and Sara to split up, Logan. Sara trusts you."

"Yeah, then why aren't we together right now?"

"Trust me, neither of you have said 'breakup,' so you're still together."

"Her not calling me, or texting me, or attempting any other form of contact is a close runner up."

"It's only been a week since the reception. Calm down."

The front door slams and the scent of rotten coconut fills the air. I fucking hate that lotion. She wears it all the time.

Abby strolls right past me, flipping through the mail.

"Don't tell me you changed your mailing address?" I ask harshly.

She pauses, glaring at me. "No, dick, I didn't. Conner asked me to grab it on the way up." She slaps the stack on the table and falls onto the couch next to Conner. He stands and looks through the mail.

"I'm waiting on that acceptance letter to the college here."

"You're going back to school?" I ask.

"Yeah, it's part of my 'I'm a fucking grown up' plan for my son's mother," he says, using quotes and rolling his eyes.

"You can just say his name." I laugh. "Jake sounds way better than 'my son.'"

"And if you say that line to her, remove the work 'fucking.' That word doesn't sound like you care enough to put in any effort," Abby chimes in.

I nod. "She has a point."

Conner chuckles and slouches onto one of the kitchen table chairs when he doesn't find what he's looking for.

"Are you going to apologize to me, Logan?" Abby whines from across the room.

"For what?"

"Being rude."

"Fuck no, and you're moving out."

Damn, this being a dick thing feels really weird. I stare at Abby while her eyes widen. *Yeah, I can't believe I just spit that out either.*

"Dude, seriously, you could have eased in to it."

I shrug. "No reason to beat around the bush."

"I'm not even going to argue right now. I have a new place to live—you guys were just easier to live with."

I roll my eyes.

I'm about to say something that I'll probably regret when my phone rings.

"Hello?"

"Logan?"

His voice makes my skin crawl and anger overwhelms me. What the fuck does he want? Taking Sara from me and turning her against me wasn't enough for him?

"Wow, you really are stupid," I snap at Liam and let out a small laugh.

"Don't hang up. I know I'm probably the last person you want to hear from, but I'm calling about Sara." He pauses, waiting for my response.

"If you're calling to tell me she picked you, I need to hear it from her."

"Whoa, man, no, that's not it all. Sara and I … we never … we aren't like that, I swear. And even if I were into her, I was never an option for her, Logan. It was always you, and she and I both know it."

I grunt. *Now he's kissing my ass.*

"If you're calling to remind me of your time together, you can call someone else," I say.

"Fuck. Okay, I'll get right to it. She's depressed, and I know she misses you. She is too proud to admit it, but I think she needs you, and I'm starting to worry about her. You should come here as soon as you can. I think it would be the best thing for her."

"If she is that upset, she'd call me. She said she would. Sorry, man, but you wasted a phone call."

"Logan, you know her better than anyone. Is she really going to call you and admit she was wrong? Or would she rather let it eat away at her until she sees you again?" He pauses. "The bar can't afford for her to be a mess, and I'm just … I guess I just want you both to be happy. I'm serious, Logan. She needs you."

It should piss me off that he has spent enough time with her to know this information, but right now, he's right. And I know exactly what I need to do.

"I'm on my way."

CHAPTER TWENTY-TWO

Sara

Just call him, Sara. Just pick up the phone, and dial his number. Tell him you were wrong and that you love him. He'll answer; he always does.

I grab my phone and stare at it, the same way I've been staring at it for the last six hours.

Why can't I call him?

The knock at my door saves me from answering my own question. I jump from my sofa and rush to the door, welcoming the distraction. It isn't until I've swung open the door and come face to face with Logan that I remember the fact I'd been crying all afternoon. *And he thinks he's into me.*

"Logan, what are you doing here?" My voice is breathy. I take a step back and my hand mindlessly begins to fix my hair and fidget with the thin shirt I'm wearing. The one from high school, the one I kept with the tear in the front and the missing buttons. His shirt.

He brushes past me and turns around. His hands land on

his hips and he pins me with a stare. "Liam called me, said I needed to get her soon and … look at you. I can't believe I waited this long. Fuck, I can't believe I believed you when you said you would call. You should have called me. I should have called you. This isn't us. We don't torture each other like this."

I calmly close the door and watch him pace the room. Just knowing he is here, makes me feel like I'm right where I need to be. He's right, we're better than this. He starts to pace faster, rubbing the back of his neck.

"I—"

"Sara, I don't know how many more times I have to say this, but I'll say it every day if I have to until we grow old and can no longer form sentences." He pauses and takes a step toward me. "You. Are. It. For. Me. You are the only person I want to be with. You are the only person I want to share my crazy unpredictable life with. You. It's always been you, Sara. I love you." He doesn't even wait for a response before his lips crash down onto mine.

"Tell me you love me, too," he murmurs into my ear before peppering kisses against my neck. "Tell me you never stopped."

"I could never stop loving you, Logan. Never." I swallow hard at my admission and at the fast work his hands are making. They touch the outside of my thighs and slowly move their way up. He stops at my hips and grips them right before he presses me into the wall. This time, there is no denying the hunger and desperation that comes from his kiss as his tongue tangles with mine intensely.

"Say it," he breathes, pulling away from my lips. His voice is deep as it sends a shiver down my spine. My body responds to his every touch. From the words, the way his eyes capture me, the way he touches me. There has never been another man for me.

"I love you."

He rips open my shirt, tearing the remaining buttons to reveal my breasts. He steps back and I come close to crumbling under his fiery gaze. When his eyes reach mine, I smile. "That shirt always looked better on you, but it looks best on the floor."

He growls and then grabs my arms, pulling me to my room. He doesn't bother closing the door and he doesn't waste time stripping out of his clothes. Once he's naked, I absorb his beautiful, bare body. My desire radiates, and he's touching me again in two strides.

Logan has never been one to stay traditional in bed. Each time with him is always a surprise, and I swear, it's like the first time every time. He may have a gentle and warm heart, but in bed, he is the perfect opposite.

The back of my legs hit the bed and Logan pushes me onto my back. "Take your clothes off." His voice is demanding and a part of me should feel threatened, but I don't. The look in his eyes tells me nothing more than his desire for me. They tell me that he missed me just as much as I missed him, and right now, all the anger we built up from our weeks apart is about to become one of the most mind-blowing experiences I'll ever have.

"You're not moving fast enough, I say as he crawls onto the bed and hovers over me. He tugs so hard that he flips my body over to my stomach. He grinds his hips into my backside and runs his hand down my sides, leaving pleasurable goose bumps in their wake. He lifts my hips and jerks my panties down in one swift move. I hear the rustle of his jeans behind me as he searches for a small foil packet, but I don't move. I want Logan, and I want him to have his way with me. I'll do anything he asks if it will take away the pain I saw in his eyes when he walked through my door.

He presses light feather kisses across my back as his warm body rests against mine. I inhale deeply at the thought of what is going to happen.

"I've missed you so much," he whispers, bites my earlobe, and then enters me slowly.

"Logan, yes—"

Lifting my hips a couple inches from the bed, he holds me there as his strokes grow deeper and slower. "You feel so fucking good." He presses into me once again, only to pull out quickly and flip me over. I'm not even able to miss his touch before he's inside me again.

Whatever happens with us, I'm never letting anyone or anything come between us again.

Logan

The feel of Sara's smooth legs wrapped around my waist will never get old. The way they slide against my hips with every thrust. The way she digs her heels in to the dip of my back, demanding that I go faster or harder. Every moan that slides up her throat and slips past her lips is like ecstasy. I'll never get over it and I'll never stop craving it.

"Logan, yes, keep doing that, harder—"

I thrust again and again until her breathing is fast and uncontrolled and I can feel her body starting to shake against mine. My hips move faster and harder until the words coming from her mouth no longer sound like words but like a woman who is having an out-of-body experience.

"Ahhh … yes!"

Her cries hit just as my release dashes though my body. Sara goes limp in my arms, and I know I've made her feel exactly how she makes me feel. There isn't anywhere in this world I'd rather be than right here, with Sara. Unless of course, if we were back home in Wyoming.

"I can't believe I was missing all that all because I was stubborn."

"I knew you were missing all that, but I also know I missed you more." I pull out of her and then pull her close to me. I press her back to my front and trail kisses over her shoulder.

"I'm sorry I acted like you were my property. You're not, and I never intended for it to come out that way. I wanted to be the one you turned to, not Liam."

"I know, and I should have talked to you when things started to get stressful."

Her hand squeezes mine.

"I also should have called you to tell you about Abby the day she showed up," I add.

"Yeah, how did she end up there anyway?"

"That was all Conner. She guilt tripped him."

Even as I say it we laugh. "Remind me again why we are still friends with her?" I ask.

"I have no idea. Maybe because she didn't always act like this and we're all secretly hoping the old Abby comes back."

We lay in silence for a while, and I'm almost asleep when I feel Sara's body twist in my arms until she is facing me. Her lips touch my cheek.

"Why didn't you want to tell me about your sister?" she asks, searching my eyes for the answer I haven't been able to give her.

"I didn't want you to see me fail at something else."

"When have you failed?"

I sigh, rolling onto my back and tucking my hand under my head. Not looking at her will help me get this out.

"I let you down when we broke up in high school. I didn't go to college right away, I never got a fancy job—"

"Those things aren't failure, Logan. That's life. Until coming here, I thought a career was the best thing for me, but our split made me realize there's something I want in this world more than success. I want you."

"Promise me, next time we decide to fight," he said, "we talk it out and we don't leave each other. And if I decide to reach out to Alexis again, you'll be the first person I tell."

"I promise I won't keep anything from you again, ever. But if we are sharing everything right now, then I should probably tell that I left last summer because my feelings for you were too intense, and that before I left, I thought I was pregnant."

My heart pounds so hard and fast I feel it my ears. If this is how I feel with her telling me about a scare a year ago, I can't imagine how she felt facing the possibility on her own.

"Next time tell me. I don't want you going through anything alone ever again."

She leans on her arm and lightly presses her lips to mine. I squeeze her close as she nuzzles her face into my shoulder.

"Now comes the part I wish I could avoid," she says.

"What's that?" I ask.

"Talking to my dad and finding out what the hell he's been

thinking the last two months. I just can't believe he would play us against each other. It makes no sense."

I believe it, but no sense in bringing it up now if she knows.

"When are you going to talk to him? Do you want me to go with you?"

Her hair brushes my chest as she shakes her head. "No, I'll invite him to lunch tomorrow since he's coming to town anyway."

I place a kiss to the top of her head. "If you need anything, I'm your man."

"I know." She giggles. "I wouldn't have it any other way."

CHAPTER TWENTY-THREE

Sara

"So, how are things going with Liam?" My father takes a seat across me, opening his menu. He's lucky that I decided to meet him for lunch. After everything I've learned about what he's been up to the past few months, I want nothing more than space from him. I want to cut him out because I still don't understand why a father would try to hurt his daughter this way. And that's the only reason I'm sitting here right now. He's my father. My heart races at his words, ready to get into it. He doesn't even know that I know and that makes me even angrier.

"They're great. He's a great guy."

"That's good to hear."

"Yep." I let the P pop as I say it and intentionally pretend to be extremely into the menu I'm holding.

I give him a side look with my added glare and watch as he flips the pages of his menu. He gazes over it and looks away when he catches me staring right back. His left brow rises.

"Is there something on your mind, Sara?"

"Nope." *Yes, this is it!* Here we go. I can't want to hear him talk his way out of this one. "What about you, Dad? Anything you want to tell me? Maybe about your plans not working out."

He closes the menu and lays it on the table in front of him. "Unless something is going to delay the opening at the Silver Tap, I'd say all my plans are going perfectly."

"Okay," I say, narrowing my eyes at him.

"Sara, what am I missing?"

"Nothing, Father."

"Father, huh? Clearly I'm not following you and we're not talking about the same thing. What's wrong?"

Our waiter comes up to take our drink order. He isn't there long enough for me to carefully craft what I'm going to say, so instead, I blurt it all out.

"What about your plan to split up Logan and me and then hook me up with Liam? Huh, what about that plan? It was a stupid plan. A horrible plan." My arms fly into the air. "Look at how well it worked out for you. Logan and I are as happy as we have ever been, and we are so far from splitting up that it's never going to happen. And I sure hope the reason you haven't brought me the Silver Tap's ownership papers has nothing to do with this plan." My chest is heaving as I rant at him, and when I notice all the people who are staring at us, I finally take a breath. They can stare all they want. I don't care.

A puzzled expression crosses his face and his forehead wrinkles. "That was not a plan of mine."

"Don't lie to me, Dad. I'm not a little girl anymore. I can make decisions on my own, and you're not going to like all of them. But Dad, you know Logan and I are the happiest when we are together. Why would you want anything else for me?"

My father takes a deep breath and then releases it slowly. He leans forward and closes his hands together over his menu. A sad smile slowly appears.

"You're right. I don't want anything else for you, but I never planned to split up you and Logan. When I met Liam in one of the classes when I was visiting the university, he was the most dedicated of the students, and when he mentioned that he would love to assist in a bar, I knew he would be a great fit. His goals in life are impressive, and yes, a part of me wanted my daughter to end up with a man like him. I may not have planned it, but the thought did cross my mind. When you agreed to hire him, I thought you might have seen the same things I saw in him. I didn't know you were going to start a relationship with Logan right before you left. And I sure didn't think it would last with you being in another state."

"Well, it did and just because it worked out doesn't excuse what you did."

"Can you really be upset that I wanted a good man for you? A man who graduated college at the top of his class, a man who comes from a family of good name and standing. Liam knows about the business world. He knows what is expected. Logan is too attached and it clouds his judgment."

I narrow my eyes at him and stand swiftly.

"Sara, sit down."

I take a deep breath, debating whether to storm out of here or finish this conversation with him. The grown up in me wins and I sit back in my seat. "You don't even know Logan. How dare you judge him and act like he's lower than the rest of us. He doesn't need to come from money or a family name. He just needs to be himself, the person he taught himself to be. If you looked at him, actually looked at him, Dad, you'd see how amazing, driven, and strong he is. He's the perfect guy for me, and you're crazy to think otherwise."

"I'm sorry, Sara. I see all those things now, which is why I brought the papers you've been waiting for." He reaches into his briefcase and pulls out a manila envelope. "I was waiting because when you moved, your relationship was at the infatuation stage, which in fact, does cloud judgment. This bar wasn't going to open if you were distracted, and if it did open with your mind focused on something else, I wasn't going to just let you take over and drive it into a hole."

He slides the yellow folder toward me. "The progress I saw last time I was here proved me wrong. With or without Logan, you will make a fine business owner."

"Dad, this is great, and I thank you for your apology, but after everything you've taught me, I still can't believe you would do this. After you apologize to Logan, too, that's when you can come find me. But until then, unless it's about work, we have nothing to talk about."

I hold my head high as I remove the envelope from the table and walk away. My lips press together as I hold in my tears. I'm still in shock that he admitted to everything. I thought I was going to have to fight and pry until my brain exploded. I was not expecting this at all. All my life my father was the one man I could count on. I trusted him as much as I trust Logan. He ruined it, and I'm not sure he'll ever get our relationship back. But an apology is good place to start.

I push through the door and keep walking toward my

apartment but stop to sit on the bench outside. I glance down the block to the Silver Tap. A couple of girls have their hands cupped against the window as they look inside. Smiles fill their faces as they walk away in my direction.

"That place is going to be so cool."

"I know. I can't wait for it to open. Having all these bars downtown within walking distance of each other is a great idea."

I watch as they continue past me and then disappear inside another business. My lips tug slightly. *It is going to be a cool bar.* If only they knew everything that went into making it happen, they might appreciate it even more.

As if he heard my thoughts, my phone begins to ring and Logan's picture flashes across the screen. I grin; just the thought of him naturally makes me happy.

"Hey you," I answer.

"Hey, beautiful, I miss you."

Logan

The sound of Sara's voice will always have a calming effect on me. Leaving her after we made up was hard. No, it was more than hard. It was completely miserable. I didn't want to go without her, but the summer is almost over and the Silver Tap opens mid-August. Two weeks away to be exact, and then Sara will be home. And I can't wait to have her in my arms again.

I'm still staring at my phone when Conner walks into the apartment.

"Dude, I'm 100 percent happy you and Sara are back together, and I hate to admit this, but I kind of missed seeing that goofy look on your face," he says and tosses his gym bag onto the counter.

"Yeah, I missed it too."

Conner chuckles and then chucks his basketball in my face. I catch it and fake tossing it back.

"You laugh now, but trust me, one day—"

"Oh no, no, no, not you too. Ethan has already tried to give me this talk, and I thank you for having so much faith in me, but until I have partial custody of Jake, no woman will be in this guy's life. Unless they're a one-night kind of thing, of course."

"Yeah, okay, we'll see if that actually happens."

"How are things with Sara's father?" Conner asks, grabbing bottled water from the fridge, casually switching the topic.

"They are on a little bit of rocky soil, but Sara loves her dad. She'll forgive him eventually."

Lunch with her father didn't end horribly, but still, unfortunately for me, that doesn't leave me in a great position to ask for his permission to marry her. Looks like I might need to be looking for another way to get that.

"Let's go shoot some hoops today. I have a feeling playing with you won't be so dramatic this time," Conner says, swinging his bag over his shoulder.

"Yeah, okay." I get off the couch. "Have you talked to your sister lately?"

"No, why, you think I spilled the beans on you getting engaged?"

"No, I was just wondering if she said anything to you about driving together for the Silver Tap's opening night, and

I was hoping to catch you beforehand to tell you not to blow it." I stare at him.

"How could I blow it?"

"By telling Kelsey I'm going to propose."

"I would never do that," he says sarcastically. "On purpose."

Conner and I head out for the gym, but I have to make one stop on the way. With all the money I've been making at the BA, I have decide to buy the diamond ring Sara deserves.

When I see Sara at the opening, I'm not letting her out of my sight. I love that woman more than anything, and I'm ready to start spending my life with her.

CHAPTER TWENTY-FOUR

Sara

I'm panicking. This should come as no surprise to anyone. But tonight is a huge deal for me. Everyone is going to be here, and I can't let anything go wrong. I survey the bar one last time. Everyone and everything looks to be in their places. Liam is behind the bar with a couple other bartenders I hired. Andi, Brit, and Lisa, another waitress I brought on board, are ready on the floor. Thank goodness Liam had great recommendations on friends to hire. I'm leaving tomorrow no matter what, and he has promised to call me with the bar's update each day. He also promised to hire more people because I told him twelve employees were not enough. Yes, tonight will be fine with six because it's only our closest friends and family coming, but still, together, we know a lot of people.

And my father will be here. Most of all, I want him to see that I can be with Logan and still run a business.

"Sara, calm down. Everything is going to be fine." Brit comes up behind me and gives me a pat on the back. "You look worried, and it's starting to freak me out."

"I'm just nervous, and it's totally normal to be nervous, right?" I nail her with wide eyes, praying she gives me the right answer.

"I thought you said you've worked in a bar before. Didn't you run the one in Wind Valley? What's so different about this one other than being in another state?" she asks from behind the bar where she's helping Liam.

Huh. I totally have done this before so she's right, I shouldn't be nervous.

"And it looks perfect, just like you." Logan's deep, tingling voice hums through my body as he steps through the door. Is it possible to love someone more every day? I can't get enough of this guy. He wraps his arms around me and his lips find my neck, immediately pressing gentle kisses against it. "You," he says and presses another kiss to my neck, "are," another kiss, "amazing." He kisses me one last time and pulls away to look into my eyes.

"Well, don't stop there," I tell him.

He half grins and his eyes sparkle. "I wasn't planning on it." He leans in, this time for my lips.

"I was talking about the amazing part." The words come out right before his lips touch mine and he laughs into my mouth.

"Did I ever tell you how cute you are?" he asks, and I can feel his warm, minty breath.

"Probably more than you should." I kiss him one more time and then step back before our make-out session is the first thing people see when they get here. I turn for the bar, and that's when I find everyone staring at me.

"What?"

A few head shakes and a shrug is all I get. And then Liam chuckles.

"Seriously, what, you guys?" My face begins to warm when smiles slowly begin to appear on all their faces.

"We've just—" Lisa begins.

"Never seen you so—" Andi adds.

"Bubbly," Brit finishes.

I turn at Logan's laughter behind me to playfully swat his arm. I don't want to be all flushed when people get here, and with everyone beaming these shocked expressions at me, I'll never get my face back to its normal color in time.

"Oh my god! This place looks amazing!" Kelsey gushes as she walks in.

"Yeah, it does," Beth chimes in behind her.

"Not bad, not bad," Ethan says, stepping up next to Kelsey and swinging his arm around her shoulders. His head nods as he glances around. "So, this is what you've been doing with all your time," he adds and then sends a wink Logan's way.

"Sara, did you hear me?" Kelsey asks behind me.

I definitely did not hear her.

"Hmmm," I say, pulling my eyes away from Logan to Kelsey.

She laughs, and Beth and Ethan are right there with her. "You two have it bad for each other. Give it up already and get married." Ethan pats Logan on the back as they continue inside, and Conner steps in their place.

He pins me with a glare and then smiles. "You did good,

Sara. Now get your butt back to Wind Valley so I don't have to watch this guy mope around anymore." Again, he pats Logan on back and heads inside.

"We have some interesting friends," I say.

"I couldn't agree more but—"

"You couldn't pick any better ones?" I fill in.

"Not at all."

Logan dips his head for a kiss and just when our lips are about to touch, my father clears his throat behind us.

"Sara, darling." He pulls me in for a shoulder hug. "Logan," he says and extends his hand.

"Mr. Connelly." Logan responds and they do that weird one firm handshake thing. They stare at each other for a moment until I clear my throat.

"The place looks wonderful, Sara, and it's been a pleasure, Logan," he says, giving him another look I've never seen before. He nods and walks right on by.

I know my father apologized and that since then, both he and Logan pretend nothing happened. But that look was—

"Stop obsessing over whatever you're thinking about and go greet the rest of your guests. I'll be around here when you're finished." Logan kisses the top of my head.

He's right. I have a bar to open.

Logan

Sara did an amazing job, and I can't believe she did all this in just ten weeks. Those also happened to be the longest ten weeks of my life, but they are over now and Sara and I have never been happier, which is why I'm planning to propose to her tonight.

After running into Sara's father at the jewelry store, where he was replacing the battery in his watch and I was buying Sara a ring, well I went for it and asked him. They guy seriously told me he'd "think about it" and "let me know." Just now, when he nodded to me in the doorway, that was his permission for me to marry his daughter. I know it was.

"Isn't this place amazing? Maybe Sara will come home and give the BA a re-opening. If this place hits it off, it might be worth the time." Ethan pats me on shoulder. He keeps doing that like he knows I'm up to something and need the encouragement. Yep, he's smirking. *Conner told him.*

"I agree, but if I'm honest, I really hope Sara is too busy planning something else for the next year." I reach my hand into my pocket and curl my fingers around the black velvet box inside, pulling it out for a glimpse. If anyone can keep me from freaking out right now, it's Ethan.

I know tonight is going to be the night I take a knee for her in front of everyone we know, but I still don't know how I'm going to do it. If I were smart, I would have the entire performance planned out to be the most romantic moment of her life. But I'm an idiot, and all I worried about was making sure I didn't lose the ring between Wind Valley and here.

"I'm confused." Ethan rubs his chin as his eyes flicker between me and the ring box. "I thought you were going to do it after the opening?"

"Nope. During."

"How?"

"Wing it. Call everyone's attention, and put her in the center of the room. I guess you'll find out."

"Hey, you remember the way I proposed to Kelsey. I had a

broken heart and I looked like a slob who hadn't showered in days. Somehow she came to my house and still said yes."

"True." I laugh with him. "These poor girls had no idea what they were getting into picking us, did they?"

"Hey guys, glad you could make it." Liam approaches Ethan and me, reaching his hand out to shake ours. He then rubs his neck before he looks directly at me. "I want to apologize for everything. I never planned to come between you and Sara. I didn't even know that was a plan for anyone until … well, you know how things went down. Anyway, man, I'm sorry and I hope we can somehow be friends."

I stare back at him, not saying anything. What can I say? After I learned Sara's father hired him as a plan to split us up and then it worked, causing our relationship to hit the rocks for a bit, I had a strong dislike for the guy. Then, Liam found out and helped me fight to get her back, so what does that leave there to be mad about? In my book, we've been friends since that moment.

"Consider yourself already part of the group, man. Anytime you're in Wind Valley, you've always got a place with us."

"Thanks, I'll definitely be taking you up on that." He shakes my hand one more time and then returns to his position for the night behind the bar. Ethan gives me one more pat on the back and then disappears to find Kelsey. I roll my shoulder. Jeez, at this rate, I'm going to have a bruise.

Suddenly, the stage is empty and the room is calming down. This is the moment I've needed all night. Everyone is paired off in couples and happier than ever. It's the perfect time to make my move. My eyes scan the room almost frantically until they land on Sara. She's standing with her father, and I'm relieved to see a smile on both of their faces. More than likely this means her father approves of the bar. I take a step toward them. My sudden movement must have caught her father's eye because he's now watching my every move. His stare is intense, but my feet keep moving. I'm not backing down now.

"Friends and family, can I please have your attention?"

My steps slow as Mr. Connelly's voice booms through the open room—the way it always does—capturing everyone's attention. A flashback of Sara's birthday party plays inside my mind. He wouldn't try to step between us again—would he?

Without a second thought, I lace Sara's fingers with my own. Her hand clenches around mine, and with that one simple movement my heart pounds inside my chest. I slip my free hand inside my pocket and open the ring box. I take the ring from its nestled spot and cradle it away from prying eyes.

"As you all know, this bar was a gift for Sara. She has put hard work and dedication into the place you are all standing in today." The crowd applauds and a few cheer in the background. They are coming from Kelsey and Beth from the sounds of it. Mr. Connelly taps the microphone to control the excitement of the room. That's the same moment I slip the diamond onto Sara's finger. I hear her sharp gasp and her hand begins to tremble. In one step I'm behind her, wrapping my arms around her entire body.

"I love you more than words can describe. I know in my heart that we are meant to grow old together, to have kids together, to love together, and to learn together. Sara Connolly, would you be my wife?" I whisper into her ear. Her body presses back against mine as she inhales.

"Sara, dear, could you please come up here?"

The entire room's attention is on us, and when she moves out of my arms, I almost pull her back.

"Sara, you have had to sacrifice a number of things to be here today. I am to blame for part of that, and I am the luckiest father to raise such a forgiving woman. I hope this is a night you'll cherish forever, and I thought it would be fun if I were able to assist in some way. Logan, can you come up here as well?"

What the—?

Silence is everywhere as I join Sara. I look to her father to see if he will hint something, anything to me right now. I have no idea what's going on and I'd really like to get back to finishing my proposal. Would it be rude to cut him off until after she says yes? His eyes match mine and he nods.

"Logan, why don't you pull out that box from inside your pocket?"

Wow. This is what he's assisting with. Weird, but kind of cool, too. I reveal the box from my pocket and the crowd immediately starts to cheer. Mr. Connelly steps back to give me this moment. I catch Sara's eye as I kneel in front of her. When she smiles and nods, it's the most beautiful moment of my life.

I turn to face our audience. "Well, I planned to grab every-one's attention and make a huge scene tonight. I wanted this moment to be special and couldn't picture any way better than to include all of you." A collective aww fills the silence. "But, I changed my mind."

"What!" Kelsey's voice rings out and Ethan plants his hands firmly on hips and glares at me. I see Sara's father take a step forward. I pop the box open and people begin to whisper when they realize it's empty.

"I already said yes!" Sara steps out and holds her hand up in the air. Cheers fall all around us, and I don't waste another minute pulling her into my arms and kissing her. Everything inside my body warms. This is the girl for me, and I couldn't be happier or more thankful in my whole life.

EPILOGUE

One month later …

Logan

I am 100 percent whipped over Sara Parker. That's right, Parker. She officially became my wife as of one hour ago. I love that not a single person thought our wedding was rushed, and I love that Sara and her father have mended their relationship. Signing full ownership of both the BA and the Silver Tap over to us was an amazing wedding gift. His including me as an owner was a huge reason she forgave him.

We made the decision to live in Wind Valley permanently. Rockland isn't too far away, but knowing it's in Liam's hands gives us peace of mind. He's a great manager and overall a person whom I've grown to trust.

The life I have at this exact moment couldn't be any better. Yes, a part of me will always wonder what it's like to have family who shares the same blood, but as long as I have Sara, nothing else matters. One day, I may search for Alexis again, but right now I'm happy with where my life is. Besides, she could still very well show up one day.

Sara's laughter from the dance floor catches my attention. I'll never get over the way she makes me feel. Like I'm important, proud, loved. She makes me want to be a better man. I told her all of this when I read her my vows, but I'll more than likely spend the rest of my life reminding her how amazing she is.

"Married life is the best life. Cheers, man." Ethan takes a seat next to me and sets a beer in front of me on the table. He tips the spout of his beer toward the dance floor. Sara is dancing with Beth and Kelsey.

I turn to tell Ethan he's right when a loud crash comes from a table behind us. Kelsey's dad is standing at the dessert table with a broken plate at his feet and a screaming baby in his arms. Ethan laughs, "Parenting, on the other hand, is beautiful but unpredictable and testing." He moves quickly to help his father-in-law. Clara cries until Ethan has her in his arms. Then it's as if nothing happened and life is good again. I want that. I want it soon, and I hope Sara does, too.

"Congrats again, Logan," Conner says, taking the seat Ethan left empty. "It's crazy how my sister and my best friend are both married now. Next thing you know, you'll have a kid."

"I sure hope you're right. If it happens sooner rather than later, maybe they can grow up with your little guy. How's he doing, by the way?"

"He's good. He's getting more comfortable with me. His mom is still being awful about all this. She now says she has no problem letting him stay with me from time to time under the condition that I get my own place. But that isn't the first thing she has asked me to do."

"What's wrong with Kelsey's place?" I ask. Until he can find his own place, Conner moved in with his sister and Ethan after Sara moved in with me.

"Nothing. Every time I do what she asks, she has another stipulation. At this rate, I'll never get him one on one."

"Things will work out. Keep your head up. Maybe what you really need is to find a woman, marry her, and then create a family that she can't say no to. A woman who also gets along with Sara and your sister would be nice."

Connor laughs, and squeezes my shoulder as he stands. "We can't all have a woman like Sara."

I grin at his words and silently pray he meets someone to help turn things around. He really is a great guy, I wish there was a way I could help, but I got nothing. This is definitely an area that could use a woman's advice.

"Logan."

I look up and can't stop my lips from the massive, all-teeth smile that takes over. "Yes, my wife?"

"Do you want to come dance with me or keep gazing at Ethan and Clara with jealousy?"

The chair I'd been sitting in shoots away from the table, and I rush around it toward her. I wrap my arms around her and lift her into the air before I kiss her.

"I'll never be jealous of anyone as long as I have you."

"Logan Parker, there's no reason to make me swoon over you now. I've already married you."

"I'll make you swoon every day for the rest of your life," I say, placing another kiss to her lips and guiding her to the dance floor.

As I hold my wife in my arms, I give a silent thank you for the life I have and for the luck I've had in love. One thing is for sure, I've never loved someone so hard in my entire life.

***

Want exclusive content delivered right to your inbox? Subscribe to Jami's mailing list for all the book news!

Are you ready for Conner and Alexis's book?

Read Just One Touch today!

JUST ONE TOUCH
CHAPTER ONE

Conner

I can and I will be a great father for my son.

"Dad! Dad! Did you see?" Jake stands in front of me, his arms swinging as he catches his breath. "I almost made it. Uncle E didn't lift me high enough."

I shoot a look toward Ethan that says *next time you make sure my kid makes the basket*, but he and our good friend Logan are too busy playing one-on-one at this point.

"Next time, bud, I bet you make it."

"I hope so! I wanna be the best like you, Dad."

I grin as he takes a juice pouch from the cooler near the driveway and sits on the grass next to me, his legs bent and arms resting by the elbows over his kneecaps, just like me.

I wanna be the best like you, Dad.

His words strike me right in the chest. I don't ever want him to think otherwise. He doesn't know that every night he isn't with me, I'm working shifts to make enough money to pay my rent because I want him to have a warm place to come home to when I have custody. I moved out of my sister's basement and into my own apartment four months ago. Rent isn't cheap.

"Where did Aunt Kelsey go?" he asks, twisting on his bum to find her. His hand holding the Capri Sun squeezes a little too tight, causing fruit punch to squirt out of the straw. The liquid lands on his cream plaid shorts. Thank God it's clear liquid and not red. Stains in clothes are not an area of my expertise. The wet spot blends right in with the dirt and grass stains he got earlier playing with his two-year-old cousin and my niece Clara, Kelsey and Ethan's daughter.

He notices the new spill and attempts to brush it off, only soaking it in more.

"She went inside to get a surprise for you. Why don't you go get Uncle E and Logan and tell them to come sit until Kelsey comes back outside?"

"Okay!" His entire face beams with excitement. His juice packet is thrown to the side as he takes off running across the driveway. I notice his untied shoelace a step too late. He hits the concrete, skidding his knee across the hard surface. I'm off the grass before he can get up. In a swift move I pick him up at the waist, place him back on his feet, and kneel in front of him. Logan and Ethan come up behind me.

"Hey, bud, what happened?" Logan asks.

"That was quiet the digger you took," Ethan says.

Jake looks between them and back to me. I can see the tears trying to fight their way out, but he's fighting harder not to cry in front of anyone right now. I stubbed my pinky toe the other day when we were at home. Jake asked why I didn't cry, and I told him it was because I'm a man and men don't cry.

He then told me he was a man, too. My heart swells and I feel like a damn sap.

He wants to be just like me.

"That's going to make a nice battle wound." Logan points to Jake's new bloody knee. "Does it hurt?"

Jake looks at me quickly before he shrugs his little shoulders. "No, I'll be fine," he says before squirming out of my hold. He starts to walk away from the circle we've made toward the side garage door. Probably to go inside where my sister is.

"How about we get it cleaned up?" I suggest. I'm sure he hasn't thought of that, but he'll pretend he has and act like he doesn't need me. A phase I hope he grows out of, soon.

"I can do it," he says without stopping and quickly is inside the house.

"You've got a tough guy on your hands these days, huh?" Logan asks, chuckling as the basketball shoots from his hands, hitting nothing but net.

"He better be tough. I'm going to need someone to look after Clara when she starts going to school," Ethan adds as he swoops up the ball from under the hoop.

"Yeah, that's a few years away, and that's also if Heather agrees to let him go to school in Wind Valley. She has till the end of the summer to decide, and I suggested making a decision sooner to help with getting the paperwork done, but that only made things worse."

"Why would she even consider him attending school in Envy? It's a small town with a school of like ten kids. If Jake went to Wind Valley, he'd have way more options in everything: sports, clubs, and academics. Plus, WV is only a twenty-minute drive from Envy. She should suck it up for Jake."

Leave it to Logan to be all about the facts. I swear, since he found out his wife, Sara, was expecting, this whole new person came out of him.

"If she picks Envy, it's only because of my lack of trying."

"Trying to what?" Logan asks.

I scratch the back of my neck as I look away. How can I explain to them that Heather has suggested dating, without getting the dead-stare look they always give me? The one that says, *I wish I could help, but I have no idea what to say right now.* "She wants to give the family thing a try," I say, summing it up quick.

Single me is screaming no every time I think about it. Father me—he doesn't want to rule out anything that could be the best decision for my son.

And, yep, right there, that's the look. The basketball stays pinned under Ethan's arms as they stare at me.

"Like, as a couple and not just Jake's parents?" Ethan asks.

"You and Heather?" Logan asks at the same time.

"Yep," I answer, nodding slowly. "That's her idea."

"The same woman who made all these crazy rules for you to follow so you could get time alone with Jake. The crazy mother who didn't want you around and wouldn't agree with anything you said?" I don't miss Logan's concern buried in the tone of his voice.

"Yeah, that's about my exact thought process," I tell him. After all, for the first two years of Jake's life, she didn't tell me I had a son. *You're irresponsible and can't even take care of yourself. There was no way I was going to put my child in your hands.*

"When did she decide this?" Ethan asks.

"About two days ago."

"Well, crap, what are you going to do?"

I shrug, because that's my only reaction to the entire idea. I still can't wrap my head around the fact she even came up with it. We were never a couple to begin with. We fooled around once, that was it. Why try now? And it's not that she isn't attractive, I just don't feel a connection with her other than Jake. I've seen the way my friends are with their wives or the way they talk about them when they aren't. I don't have that for Heather.

"I don't want to say I'm 100 percent against the idea, but forcing feelings for someone and then it not working out doesn't sound like anything that ends well."

"Do you think you could have feelings for Heather?" Logan asks.

"Maybe. I mean, we fooled around one night and now this is where we end up. I haven't really made much of an effort to get to know her outside of who is doing what for Jake."

"So you think if you get to know her, you might develop real feelings for her?" Ethan asks this time.

"There's only one way to find out, right? If it means giving Jake a good life, I should try anything."

"Well, I guess there's your answer," Logan says.

"Yeah, I suppose you're right."

"And you know, if you need to talk or maybe get a woman's perspective without leading Heather on, Kelsey might be able to help," Ethan adds.

I nod—my sister would be the right person to talk to about

this— but Heather is really who I should go to. Communication is what will make this work the best.

I pull my cell from my pocket to shoot her a text asking if we can meet for ice cream before my shift at the BA tonight.

The garage door opens and Clara steps out in a blue and white polka dot dress, her brown hair looking a bit ratty from a day of playing with her cousin. Her steps are slow as she focuses on the paper bowl in her hands with a scoop of ice cream in it. Jake comes out next, his steps just as cautious for the same reason and a bandage over his knee. Then Kelsey pokes her head out, holding the door open enough to show a glimpse of her seven months' baby bump.

"I have a bowl for each of you, if you want to come get it."

You don't have to tell us twice.

Once we've all settled down in the grass and eaten our ice cream, I glance at my watch. I told Heather we could meet in an hour.

"Jake, why don't you head on over to Grandma and Grandpa's and give them a hug goodbye?" With them living across the street from my sister, it's easier to visit everyone when we come here.

"Do I have to leave?" His tiny, sad voice breaks my heart.

"Yeah, bud, your mom misses you the way I do when you're gone." I ruffle his head and mess up the same chocolate-brown hair that I have in the process.

I can't read the blank expression on his face, but based on his resistance to move right now, I don't want to know what he's thinking.

My little man stops at the sidewalk and looks both ways before he crosses the street. At four years old, he should be by my side for this journey, but with it being a slow neighborhood, the group of us observing from the grass and my parents, standing on their porch, I think he's just fine crossing on his own.

He gives them each a hug and then repeats his process back across the street. A few more hugs later, we're in my truck and headed back to my apartment. I only glance in the rearview mirror a few times, because the bummed out look on his face is heartbreaking. I don't want him to go either, and if I could say anything to him without tearing up myself, I'd want him to know that I'm fighting for him. To be a part of his life, to make sure he is always taken care of.

Being a family could give me all that.

I pull up in front of my apartment building. It has the exact same four-plex layout as Sara and Logan's, only this is in the building next to theirs. Still, it's walking distance from my job at the Black Alcove Bar and I love it.

I put the gear of my red, four-door Ford truck into park and take notice of the moving truck out front and the small, white Corolla that's in my usual parking spot. There is a heart sticker in the window with the number 26.2 in the center. That can only mean one thing. The new tenant, the one moving in across the hall from me, is crazy and a runner. All runners are crazy in my opinion. What a boring sport.

"Hey, bud, let's keep the secret of you having ice cream at Aunt Kelsey's house between us, okay?" I say, catching his attention in the rearview mirror. Heather would not be too impressed if she knew he ate ice cream twice in one day when he's staying at her place tonight. Bedtime will be fun for her.

My bad.

"Why?" he asks.

"If we keep it a 'Daddy and me' secret, maybe we can do it again someday," I reply instantly, because I knew that he would ask why. His eyes light up and he nods numerous times.

With a shake of my head, I turn off the engine and hop out, opening Jake's door just in time for him to jump out, too. He thinks he's cool because he can unhook his seat belt and doesn't need his dad to do it, but one time he did it too soon was all it took for him to learn it's even cooler to wait until the truck is turned off before he pulls on the buckle.

He doesn't say anything, but he peeks inside the white truck, taking note of the fact that only a few boxes and a chair are left to move.

"That looks like our chair, Dad." Jake points right before he starts to climb in, but I tug him back by his back belt loop.

"That's not our stuff, bud. Let's go inside, alright? I'm just going to grab the mail and I'll meet you in there. Wait for me once you're inside."

He nods fast, walking straight for the doors like I taught him. *Don't stop for anyone.*

I watch him the entire time until his little body is completely inside. The mail contains just another power bill and an issue of *American Motorcyclist*. I tuck both pieces under my arm as I open the door. I expect to find Jake standing in front of our apartment door, quietly waiting for me, because that's our agreement during this phase, but he isn't. He's standing in front of the door across the hall, talking to our new neighbor instead.

"Yeah, and then my Uncle E"—deep breath—"he picked me up and I didn't make it." He takes another deep breath as he finishes giving what I'm guessing is the quickest rundown of his afternoon.

My mouth is half open, ready to start in on my "what did I tell you about talking to strangers?" talk when I take the last step inside the building, allowing his chatter companion to come into view.

Long and tan legs, toned from what I'm going to assume is a crap load of running, stand before me in a pair of cut-off jean shorts and a black Nirvana t-shirt that hugs a perfect rack. Blonde hair is pulled up into a messy, sexy-as-hell bun on top of her head with a few wisps of hair falling down her face. Crystal clear eyes like diamonds with just a hint of blue in the center catch my gaze, and I'm completely drawn to them. When she smiles, any lecture I'm about to give is fully forgotten.

"Hi, I'm Alex." Her eyes are trained on me as her grin stays put.

"Conner," I reply, grinning back, and that's when I realize there is a dresser, a mattress, and multiple boxes blocking our apartment door. This isn't a very big entryway. I don't even know how they got all this in here. I check my watch again.

"Are they going to be much longer to move this?" I ask, pointing to all the stuff in front of my door.

"Dad, is she our new neighbor?" Jake tugs on my hand.

"No," she says, peering out the front door behind me. "They said they were taking a quick break, though."

"A quick break? I have somewhere I need to be." Heather likes promptness. Showing up late isn't in the plans for me.

"Oh," is all she says, followed by a forced frown and shrug. "Maybe you could get inside through a window?"

"A window?" She can't be serious. Her response tells me she doesn't care about the inconvenience she's causing me. "You think I should take my son and break into my own apartment through a window?

"Or you just cool down and wait. It was just a suggestion." Her stance changes as her hip pops to the left and she crosses her arms.

My left brow cocks at the fact that she actually seems irritated by *me*. I'll just take care of it myself. I may be overreacting, but if her attitude right now is any indication of what kind of uncaring neighbor is moving in across the hall from me, I'm not thrilled, and the less interaction we have, the better.

I grab a box and turn for her apartment. She cuts me off before I make it through the doorway, and I have to take a deep breath before I lose that so called "cool" she thinks I need to find. I need in inside my apartment if we're going to meet Heather on time and I refuse to wait for her or her worthless movers to move all of this junk. Whether she likes it or not, I'm doing it myself.

Alexis

"What do you think you're doing?" I ask, pulling my view from the bulging biceps that are tugging against his shirt as he holds one of my boxes in front of him. Typical guy, taking charge of the situation, like a girl doesn't have the aggression to do it herself.

"I don't have time to wait on your lazy movers," he says, nudging me with the box to move out of his way.

"Put my things down." I push back against the cardboard. This guy can't just walk in here and tell people what to do or be rude for no reason. It wasn't like I told my movers to put my stuff in front of his door so I could have a rocky start with a new neighbor. Being in this town has my nerves on edge enough as it is.

"Just let me move your shit," he says.

"Dad, you said a bad word!"

"Jake, sit on the steps while Dad helps move this lady's things, okay?"

Great, I have a neighbor who thinks he owns the place and can do whatever he wants with my stuff.

"That won't be necessary because you aren't touching any of my shit," I say, and immediately cringe that I just swore in front of his little boy.

Conner, I think he said his name is, rolls his eyes and then nudges me again. This time I try to yank the box out of his grip. He doesn't let go, so I do it again.

"Fine," he growls at the same time I give up, thinking he isn't giving up, but I am wrong. The box drops, shattering the moment it meets the floor. Oh my god, I'm going to kill him. He had better hope that wasn't valuable. I kneel to the floor, flipping one tab of the box open, my eyes find the broken frame and tears fall immediately. The clay frame my brother made me before we were split into two different fosters homes is broken into pieces.

"Look, I didn't—"

"You should have just listened to me!" I stand and push the box into my apartment with my foot.

"I was just trying to help you," he argues.

"I didn't ask for your help!" I yell again as more tears come. I turn, prepared to slam my door in his face and hopefully hit him with it in the process when two small eyes grab my attention. His son is staring right at me, blinking and looking ready to cry as well. I sniffle and take a deep breath before I calmly close my door.

I let out a couple more slow breaths and slide down the door, sitting next to the box. I pull out the pieces of the frame, running my fingers over the sharp edges of the blue, green, and yellow pieces. Next I pull out the faded photo that used to being inside it and choke back more tears when I notice a corner stuck to part of the frame, leaving it ripped.

My last memory of my brother, Logan, is of when we were making these picture frames in the children's home, before they separated us. It was like he knew they couldn't keep us together. He was hugging me, telling me to be brave, that I was the strongest little girl he knew, and that no matter what, I'd see him again one day. For some reason, this frame and the fact I kept it in good condition gave me hope that his words were true.

Now it's broken and I hope I never run into my jack-hole of a neighbor ever again and coming to Wind Valley has been the worst decision I've ever made.

* * *

Yoga has always been my go-to when I'm stressed, and since I'd applied for a job at this gym before I moved here, I knew they offered classes. Between my afternoon and plotting how, if, or when I tell my brother I'm here, it seemed liked the right thing to do. This class, however, wasn't what I expected.

The lights flick on as the class comes to an end, and the redhead next to me keeps talking. This would usually annoy me, considering this is a class of peace, but she sounds friendly enough and somewhere in her chat session—where she did the majority of the chatting—she actually invited me out for a drink tonight. Since I don't know anyone, it sounds like a pretty great idea.

"Okay, so the bar is called The Black Alcove, have you heard of it?" she asks, spraying down her yoga mat and passing me the bottle.

"I think it's near my apartment," I answer honestly, even though about eight percent of me isn't sure that's the same bar I saw earlier.

"You think?" she laughs. "Where do you live?"

"In the Hillman Apartments on Center Street."

The redhead stops rolling her mat and her eyes go wide as she looks at me.

"Seriously! That's in the building next to mine!"

This time it's me who pauses mid-roll. It's always hard moving to a new place, especially alone. My fear is that at twenty-one you've hit that awkward age where either you have all the friends you need or you're making new friends in college, so if you don't have any, people think there's something wrong with you. Seeing as college isn't something I want to do right away, I've been dreading that I'll end up as option three. Only the redhead here doesn't seem to have the same plan for me. I should probably ask her name.

"Well, neighbor, how about we actually introduce ourselves? I'm Alex." Like I was taught at a young age, I offer my hand and present her with a smile. She laughs it off but doesn't shake my hand.

"You're one of those polite, fancy girls, aren't you?" She eyes me, tucking her mat into her bag. "You're from the south. I hear the catch of an accent."

"Yeah, North Carolina."

"How in the heck did you end up in Wyoming?"

She isn't looking at me now, which is good. She seems like the outspoken type and I've been told I have a "give-away" face. People always know what I'm thinking with just one look. And right now, I worry she might see the real answer and not accept the one I tell people, because once people learn you grew up in the foster system, they look at you differently. Most people don't realize they're doing it, looking at you with pity. Besides, I think telling someone I grew up without my real family and I came here to find my real brother might be a bit much for day one, or any day, really.

"Just trying something new." I shrug. I've got my yoga mat against my hip and my water bottle dangling from my finger as I wait for her.

"You know, I have a hunch the blonde girl in the corner was new, too, because in this town almost everyone knows everyone and I do not know her. That, and college kids won't be rolling in a for a few more months, sooo, where is she?" Red hair whips her neck around as she surveys the room. Her back straightens when she finds who she's looking for.

"Hey you," she hollers at a thin, pale blonde across the room. "Are you new here?"

The girl nods hesitantly, as though it caught her off guard

that someone would actually be talking to her. I know the look because I used to give it all the time.

"Are you twenty-one?"

The girl nods again.

"Fantastic, come have a drink with us tonight. My other girlfriends are all married with kids now; I need a couple new single gals. What's your name?"

"Skylar," the blonde answers, still seeming a little unsure of my new redheaded friend. Crud, what is her name?

"And you are?" I ask, urging her one more time to share her name.

"Beth." She laughs. "Sorry I got a little sidetracked when you asked me earlier."

I notice how Skylar returns her mat to the pile of borrowed ones, and then she thanks the instructor. Beth and I thank her as well before we step out in the hallway where cool air brushes against my skin now wet from sweat.

"Alright, so let's all go home and shower and meet at the BA in about an hour?" Beth looks between me and Skylar. It's actually cute that she is all about this new friend thing. I want to know more about these friends she used to hang around, but without knowing whether it's a sore subject or not, I better not.

"Alex, we can walk together if you want. Skylar, do you know where to go?"

Skylar nods and then turns for the locker room while Beth and I head for the exit. We part ways, and as I drive to my new apartment, I mentally cross my fingers that I don't reveal too much during drinks. Sharing little pieces of your life with a new friend is usually what happens when you meet someone new. And no one wants to know that, for years, I'd thought my family didn't want me. That's why I was in the foster system, right? Because someone didn't want to be my parent or devote enough of their time to me.

At this time, letting anyone in on this secret is not something I want to do. I have no idea why I was ready to move to another state but not ready to admit to anyone that I'm really here. That gut-aching feeling that there could be a chance he's changed his mind won't go away, and until it does, this is my secret to keep.

I take a quick shower and dry my hair before putting on a pair of jeans with holes down the front—sadly they weren't made that way, but I've managed to alter them to at least look fashionable—and a new t-shirt. It's only June and I've only been here since this morning, but I swear I've already gone through the chilly morning, a warm and misleading afternoon, and now, it's turning into a windy evening. The weather here can't seem to make up its mind.

I steal a glance at the clock on my phone. I told Beth I'd meet her outside about forty-five minutes after we left the gym. It's about that time, and although I should stay home to unpack some things, I rush out the door to find her standing on the sidewalk, chatting away on her phone. She, too, is wearing a pair of jeans, only hers are sans the holes and she's got on a green hoodie that makes her red hair even brighter than before.

"Perfect timing because I am starving," she says dramatically, but in a fun way. I'm learning that Beth is one of those beautiful outspoken women. The kind that are unaware of how attractive they are. Not that I'm attracted to her, but her personality is attractive, and that I do enjoy. I sort of hope a bit of her bluntness can rub off on me one day.

We walk to the bar, passing the time with small chitchat—age, birthdays, music, all the random things. She's twenty-four while I'm twenty-one. Her birthday is in January, mine is in October, both on the twenty-third of the month, which we find pretty coincidental. And we both feel the same about music: as long as it's good, the genre doesn't matter. It isn't until we've reached the bar that she tells me she also works here, so I shouldn't be thrown off when every employee stops by the table to say "hey."

Only two tables are open when we arrive, and there isn't a spot open at the bar. Beth rushes to a booth, motioning for me to follow her.

"It's still early, but the burgers here are to die for. Once people eat their dinner, it will die down till the evening rush," she tells me, sliding a menu my way.

I'm about to open it when the door opens and Skylar walks in. Like earlier, she hesitates before she steps inside. When she catches the sight of Beth's hand waving in the air to gain her attention, she heads right for our table without even a glance at anyone as she passes them.

"Thanks for inviting me," she says, taking a seat next to Beth. "I actually ate right before yoga, so I hope it's okay that I just came to hang out. I don't really know anyone here." She starts to bite her nails, looking nervously back and forth between Beth and myself.

"I just moved here, too. Today actually," I say, hoping to calm her nerves. Her hand drops and she sits up a little straighter.

"Oh, you two are cute." Beth laughs. "If you want to know people, I can help you with that. But first, pick out some food so we can order."

We sit in silence as we each look over the menu. I haven't read even two items before three different people stop by to say hi. Beth doesn't introduce us to any of them. I guess these aren't the people she wants us to know.

"Hey, Beth," a small female with a blonde and brown fade says as she stops at our booth.

"Abby." Beth doesn't even glance up to look at her.

Abby stands there, not acting offended as she offers both me and Skylar a fake smile. It's a little awkward.

"Can I get you something to drink?"

"I'll just have water," Skylar says quickly.

"Can I have a Roy Rogers?" I ask. Abby stares at me while Beth laughs.

"I thought we were coming out for a drink. Water and a Roy Rogers are not what I meant."

"Hey, I need to eat first," I say and this seems to an acceptable answer. Beth orders a Redds' Apple Ale, and the moment Abby shifts away from the table, I have a direct view of the bar. More specifically, of the guy standing behind the bar. It's my neighbor. He's on my shit list for breaking the only thing I had left to remind me of my brother, but right now I'm realizing something else: there is a stupid crazy hot guy living next door to me and I can't pull my eyes away. He flashes a smile at the two women in front of him and then he winks. His gaze lifts, finding mine. With a tilt of his head and another cute-as-hell grin, he waves at me.

"Oh, I see you've found Conner," Beth says.

"The guy behind the bar?" I ask, trying to sound uninterested.

"That's the one. If he weren't my best friend's little

brother, I'd probably look at him with lust-filled eyes the way you are now."

"I am not." I laugh off her comment.

"It's true, and I think the fact he has a son he spends almost every free moment with makes women even more interested."

"Jake?" I ask, thinking of the little brown-haired boy I met earlier today.

"How did you know?" Beth asks.

"I met him earlier today."

"Oh that's right, you two are neighbors. Well, dang, I bet things around here are about to get pretty interesting."

"Why?" I ask, my eyes searching him out once again. But he's gone now. It's for the best. I shouldn't be checking him out. Where there is a cute guy and a kid, there is mother and significant other. I'm many things—a runner, a reader, a dreamer, even a hopeless romantic—but a home-wrecker, I am not.

"I'm no guy, but if I had a girl like you living across from me, practically there when I came home at night, I'd try to do something about it."

"Oh," I laugh her comment off once again. "I'm not in that place right now." It's true. This isn't the time for me to be starting a relationship with anyone. I mean, I've grown up in multiple foster homes, and each time I thought I found my place, they up and rejected me, placing me in a new home. Trust in the everyday human isn't something I have, and if I can't even put it in this brother who is looking for me, as much as I want to, I sure as heck know I can't put it in this random guy who already has a family. Why am I even thinking about this? Being hot is no excuse for having no manners. Which, after our encounter earlier, he is clearly lacking.

"Seriously? When isn't a girl in the place for a hot guy?"

"I've just got some other things going on my life right now that don't have place for a guy. Especially one who is—"

"Smoking hot," Skylar says, reminding me she's at the table, too.

Beth is about to object to me or agree with Skylar, I assume, when a tall figure appears at our table. My attention is pulled to focus on him. He has these dark forest-green eyes that I've never seen before but would be perfectly fine looking at for the rest of my life. My heart beats faster as I continue to check him. Dark hair just long enough to run your hands through. Strong, defined cheekbones with dark, perfectly shaved facial hair makes him look dreamy. All features I must have missed earlier in the hallway.

His chest rises and falls, grabbing my attention. The black t-shirt he's wearing reads The Black Alcove in white letters just about the chest pocket. I try to keep my attention here instead of near his eyes, because the heated look he's flashing my way right now is exciting something inside me.

"Ladies," he says, now sharing his grin with the rest of the table. "Beth, I didn't realize you had more friends." There's a joking tone to his voice that I find adorable. *No. No, I don't find it adorable.*

"Ha funny, Conner, this is Skylar." Skylar waves but doesn't look up. "And you already know Alex."

"Well, I met her briefly today, yes." He switches his gaze from hers to mine. "I actually came over here to apologize. I'm sorry about earlier, and I hope you got everything else moved in okay."

"I did, thank you," I answer, managing to turn my gaze to a plastic beer advertisement on the table.

"Actually, she was just telling me how she needs to move some furniture around, but some pieces are too heavy. Since you're her neighbor, you might be able to help."

I don't need to be looking at myself to know that my eyes have grown and my jaw is hanging open slightly at the lie. Her brow rises as she tilts her head toward Conner. I've changed my mind—Beth's bluntness isn't an admirable trait.

"I'd be happy to help," Conner says before I can correct her.

"That's really not necessary. I'll be fine."

"Well, it's not like I have to go out of my way. I get off around ten tonight, and if that's too late I can come by tomorrow afternoon."

"Tomorrow afternoon. We already have plans after this," Beth adds quickly, taking a notepad out of Conner's pocket and writing something down. Hopefully, this said cheeseburger.

"I'll see you tomorrow, then." His eyes have found mine once again, leaving me speechless. I nod as he walks away.

"Yeah, okay, I'm just going to say right now, with that dreamy look on your face, that place you're in … well, I think it just opened up a spot for Conner. Oh, and after we eat, we're all going to your place because that furniture isn't going to misplace itself."

"Where were you when I was in high school?" Skylar smiles as she plays with the napkin her water is sitting on. "And whatever he did, with a smile like his, I'd have forgiven him already."

The two quickly go into high-school talk. I shrug off the topic of my neighbor, because, if anything, I really do need help moving my TV stand and I guess I should make nice if I'm going to continue living here. I don't have to even make friends with him, just be polite is all. Conner and I are nothing but neighbors.

* * *

Finish reading Just One Touch today!

Want more from Jami?
Subscribe to her mailing list for exclusive bonus epilogues and all the book news!

MORE BOOKS BY JAMI ROGERS

The Black Alcove Series

Just One Kiss

Just One Night

Just One Touch

Just One Moment

Just One Spark

Just One Love

The Kiss Me Crazy Series

Kiss Me Crazy

Love is Crazy

I Want Crazy

The Evergreen Brothers Series

A Boyfriend by Christmas

The Summer Wedding Hoax

A Match by Christmas

The Lust or Bust Series

The Write One

Write About You

The Write Choice

Write That Down

More Than Write

Always Been Write

Standalone Novels

Love Money

Date in the Dark (A New Years Eve Novella)

ACKNOWLEDGMENTS

I will never forget the amount of support and encouragement that went in to writing Sara and Logan's story.

Mom, Dad, and Holly: You are my biggest fans, and I love you more and more each day. Thank you for believing in me and being there when I need you.

Dana Volney: In the time I've known you, we've come a long way. You motivate me, you push me, and because of you my goals actually happen. Thank you for keeping me on track.

Mary Billiter: I miss you. I wish you were here to share all these happy moments, because I know without you and the push you gave me in the beginning, my life would be so much different.

Grant Rogers: You are a trooper and I will be forever thankful to have you in my life during everything I'm going through.

Mallori Roth, Kate Maxwell, and Megan Phillips: My beta readers rock! You've all helped me and made me a stronger writer. Thank you!

Alyssa Williamson and Trisha Butcher: Thank you all for being the best girlfriends a girl could ask for and for understanding when I can't make every girls night out.

Julie Sturgeon: I love working with you. You take away

stress like it's nobody's business. Thank you for working with me!

And finally, thank you to the readers, bloggers, and social media fans who have read *Just One Night* and are spreading the word. Your support is the best thing I could ask for.

ABOUT THE AUTHOR

My name is Jami Rogers and I write new adult contemporary and adult contemporary romance novels. I *love* love and want to share my passion for happily ever afters with the world.

I was born in Wyoming and still live in the cowboy state with my husband, daughter, and two dogs. I like to read, write, run, watch movies/TV and spend time with my family. I'm horrible at returning phone calls and prefer to text, but still struggle to hit the little blue arrow to send a message once I'm finished typing my reply. My husband does 90% of the cooking in our house. Not because I'm busy – I'm just simply a bad cook.

Keep up with Jami by visiting her website www.
authorjamirogers.com
or
Subscribe to her mailing list for exclusive bonus epilogues
and all the book news!

www.ingramcontent.com/pod-product-compliance
Lightning Source LLC
Chambersburg PA
CBHW020024310726

48970CB00007B/2194